"Could I clear the air between us?"

"What do you mean?"

"About the past," Lukas replied.

Juliane's stomach sank, and her heart raced. She swallowed hard. "What about it?"

He took a deep breath. "I wanted to apologize for anything I may have done to offend you back then, and to let you know that I've changed."

"I can see that."

"But you're not sure."

She bit her lower lip. "Am I that transparent?"

He smiled. "Just a little. From the moment I met you again at choir practice the other night, I sensed that you had some big reservations where I'm concerned."

Juliane knew she had to tell the truth. "Yeah... maybe some."

"That's what I thought." He sighed. "When you told me you remembered me from your college years, I knew I probably hadn't impressed you—at least not in a good way."

"Are you trying to make me say bad things about you?"

Books by Merrillee Whren

Love Inspired

The Heart's Homecoming
An Unexpected Blessing
Love Walked In
The Heart's Forgiveness
Four Little Blessings
Mommy's Hometown Hero
Homecoming Blessings
*Hometown Promise

 *Kellerville

MERRILLEE WHREN

is the winner of the 2003 Golden Heart Award for best inspirational romance manuscript presented by Romance Writers of America. In 2004, she made her first sale to Steeple Hill Books. She is married to her own personal hero, her husband of twenty-nine years, and has two grown daughters. She has lived in Atlanta, Boston, Dallas and Chicago, but now makes her home on one of God's most beautiful creations, an island off the east coast of Florida. When she's not writing or working for her husband's recruiting firm, she spends her free time playing tennis or walking the beach, where she does the plotting for her novels. Merrillee loves to hear from readers. You can contact her through her Web site at www.merrilleewhren.com.

Hometown Promise
Merrillee Whren

Steeple
Hill®

Published by Steeple Hill Books™

STEEPLE HILL BOOKS

Steeple
Hill®

ISBN-13: 978-0-373-81458-9

HOMETOWN PROMISE

Copyright © 2010 by Merrillee Whren

www.SteepleHill.com

Printed in U.S.A.

Recycling programs
for this product may
not exist in your area.

Sustain me according to your promise, and I will
live; do not let my hopes be dashed.
Uphold me, and I will be delivered; I will always
have regard for your decrees.
                    —*Psalms* 119:116-117

I would like to dedicate this book to my wonderful agent, Pattie Steele-Perkins.

Once again, I would like to thank my daughter Danielle for being my first reader.

Chapter One

Harsh memories flashed through Juliane Keller's mind as she stopped in the middle of the church aisle. The subject of those memories—Lukas Frey—stood with members of the choir on the stage at the front of the sanctuary. Why was he here?

Brushing snowflakes from her coat, she could think of only one good reason—his wonderful singing voice. But the Lukas she'd known eleven years ago would never have used his voice to sing in a church choir. Light-headed, she grabbed the back of a pew and watched him converse with her cousins Carrie and Val. Tonight was the first official practice of the musical they were performing for Winter Festival at the end of January. Strangers weren't supposed to be there.

What was she to make of his sudden appearance in her little hometown of Kellersburg, Ohio?

With everyone absorbed in conversation, no one had noticed her entrance. Could she escape before Lukas became aware of her presence? She wanted to avoid Lukas, who dredged up things better forgotten, until she had a chance to find out what he was doing in town.

She crept backward down the aisle. She hoped her slow, quiet steps would guard her from detection. As she eased away from the stage, she bumped into someone. Letting out a yelp, she turned and came face-to-face with Tom Porter, the music minister, a rotund man with graying brown hair.

Tom grabbed her shoulders. "Juliane, are you all right? Didn't mean to startle you."

"I'm fine."

"That's good. We've been waiting for you. I'm glad you finally made it."

Trying to smile, Juliane knew everyone, including Lukas, was looking at her. "I got stuck at the store doing some last-minute stuff for my dad. Sorry I'm late."

"That's okay. Now that you're here, we can get started." Tom gestured toward the front and hurried up the aisle.

Heat creeping into her cheeks, Juliane followed Tom, keeping her eyes on the blue tweed carpeting that matched the padding on the pews. She didn't dare look at Lukas, who appeared, at least from a distance, not to have changed much in the eleven years since she'd last seen him. He was still tall and lean with coal-black hair. Was his personality the same? There was no way to tell. At least he seemed to be sober—for now. She shuddered as she recalled her last brush with a drunken Lukas Frey. Was he remembering the same thing? She hoped not.

But why was she worried? He probably didn't even remember her or their last encounter. As a college freshman, she'd barely been a blip on his graduate student radar.

When Tom reached the three steps leading to the stage, he stopped and turned to Juliane. "I want you to meet the newest member of the choir."

Juliane kept her gaze focused on Tom as her stomach churned. Lukas? A new member of *their* choir? How could that be? He didn't even live here. Besides, she had a hard time believing he was involved with a church, much less the choir. He hadn't exactly been the churchgoing type.

How should she handle this situation? Should she pretend not to know him? God expected her to tell the truth, but she was sorely tempted to lie. If only she'd been able to get away.

She forced another smile. "Who?"

"Lukas, come meet Juliane." Tom motioned for Lukas to join them.

Glancing their way, Lukas grinned. As he made his way across the stage, his gaze met hers. She remembered those startling blue eyes. They made her shiver, but relief washed over her when no recognition showed on his face. He didn't remember her. Her concern was for nothing.

Why would he remember her anyway? They'd only met in passing at a few different theater department productions. When she'd first encountered him at rehearsals, she'd wondered why someone in an MBA program would be involved in the theater group. She soon learned he was dating a graduate assistant in the theater department.

He'd been hard to miss with his handsome face, those blue eyes and dark hair. But his constant drinking had disgusted her, so she'd avoided him until the night her cousin Nathan had asked her to do a good deed by giving Lukas a ride home. As she pushed the memories away, he came down the steps and extended his hand.

"Hi, I'm Lukas Frey."

Offering him her hand, Juliane tried to keep her lips from quivering as she held her smile in place. "I'm Juliane Keller."

He narrowed his eyes. "Have we met before? Somehow you seem familiar. My grandfather lives here. Have we run into each other in town?"

Juliane digested that bit of information while an easy lie formed in her mind. He would never know the difference if she led him to believe they'd met here. But no matter the cost, she couldn't give in to the temptation. "Yes, we've met before, but not here. We met when we worked on the same theater department musical. As I recall, you were in grad school, and I was a freshman."

"How could I not remember you?"

What was that supposed to mean? Did he suddenly recall their last meeting? Doubtful. Maintaining her smile was getting painful, but she'd have to be cordial and pretend that meeting him wasn't setting her nerves on edge. "Are you visiting your grandfather?"

"Not exactly. I've moved here."

Realizing the stupidity of her question, Juliane shook her head. Lukas had her mind in a dither. "Since Tom said you're in the choir, I should've known that. Welcome to Kellersburg. I hope you and your family will enjoy living in our great little town."

"No family here except my grandfather. He moved here a couple of years ago when he retired. He wanted to get out of the city." Lukas smiled wryly. "And if I need a taste of city life myself, Cincinnati's not far away."

"Do I know your grandfather?"

Lukas shrugged. "I don't know. His name is Ferdinand Engel."

"I don't recall meeting him."

Tom jumped into the conversation. "Lukas will be in charge of running the new plant in town."

"You mean the medical devices plant?" Lukas certainly must have changed since his grad school days. Years before, he hardly seemed like someone who could handle the responsibilities of a plant manager or responsibilities of any kind. Was he truly more trustworthy now...or had he just gotten better at hiding his drinking problems?

"Yes, I'll be supervising the start-up, then the day-to-day operations."

"Are you living with your grandfather?"

Chuckling, Lukas shook his head. "Grandpa wouldn't have that, so I did the next best thing. I purchased a house in the same block where he lives. Grandpa thinks he can take care of himself, but I took this job specifically to keep an eye on him. His health's been poor in recent years."

Juliane hoped the surprise didn't show on her face. She'd never expected him to be the type who would care for a grandparent. "So you took the job here to be close to him?"

"Sort of. I've worked for this company for several years. It's a good promotion for me, and it gives me the opportunity to look after him."

Tom clapped Lukas on the back. "I had no idea you two had met before. This will give you a chance to renew your acquaintance."

"Certainly." Juliane stifled a groan. She didn't want to renew anything with Lukas Frey, but somehow she managed to smile again. By this time, her smile surely looked disingenuous. How long could she keep up this pretense?

Lukas turned to Tom. "I didn't mean to take up so much time talking. I know you want to get started."

"No problem." Tom hopped onto the stage and picked up a stack of booklets. "Okay, everyone, these contain the music score and speaking parts. You can follow along while we listen to the recording of the program and get an idea of how it goes."

Hurrying up the steps, Juliane took a booklet from Tom, hoping to distance herself from Lukas. "Are we supposed to sing with the recording or just listen?"

"We're not concerned about actually singing tonight, but if you want, you can sing along, especially those of you who have solos like you and Lukas." Tom turned toward Lukas as he joined them on the stage, then added, "Those of you with speaking parts can underline your part in the booklet."

Juliane's mind buzzed as she settled on the front pew in the choir loft. Lukas had a solo? How had that happened so quickly? She glanced at Lukas. "What part do you have?"

"I have the male lead. I think the character's name is Dave." Lukas stared at her. "How about you?"

"I've got the part of Grace, the female lead." Juliane didn't want to believe it. How had Lukas wound up with the lead male role? Her cousin

Nathan was supposed to have that. Sometime tonight she needed to have a talk with Tom and find out why the change had been made.

Smiling, Lukas sat at the other end of the pew. "Great. Then we'll be singing together."

Yeah. Great. That wasn't the word she'd use to describe the situation. Thankfully, before she could respond, Tom turned on the recording.

While they listened to the songs, Juliane couldn't concentrate on her part, especially when she realized how much interaction David and Grace had in the musical. That meant lots of interaction between Lukas and her. Could she get someone else to take her part? That would solve the problem.

Juliane dismissed that idea instantly. Maybe God was trying to remind her that His love extended to everyone—even people who sometimes seemed unlovable. Dealing with Lukas was definitely a test of her resolve to be Christ-like.

Besides, she'd been looking forward to this year's program for the Winter Festival and the opportunity to tell the story of God's love not just to church-goers but also to the community at large. She wanted to use her voice for God's glory. Now she had to put God's love into practice by being nice to Lukas even though she didn't relish the idea.

When she glanced up from the music score, Lukas was looking at her. He didn't seem embarrassed to be caught staring. His audacity hadn't changed in eleven years. Had anything else?

She'd been at a cast party on that night eleven years ago when she'd looked out the window to see Lukas headed for his car, keys in hand. She couldn't let him drive home after all he'd had to drink at the party. He'd kill himself or someone else. How could she stop him?

As she'd turned to find help, her cousin Nathan approached. She hurried over to him and explained the situation.

"You're right. We can't let him drive." Without waiting for her, Nathan raced out the door.

Juliane followed him into the night. She caught up to him just as he reached Lukas, who was still fumbling to unlock his car.

Nathan put a hand on Lukas's shoulder. "Having a problem?"

"Yeah, man." Lukas looked up, a silly grin on his face.

Nathan reached for the keys. "Let me see what I can do."

Juliane sighed with relief when Lukas handed over his keys without resistance. Nathan unlocked the car.

"Hey, man. Thanks." Lukas leaned against the car still grinning like a fool. "Now I can go home."

"I can't let you drive," Nathan said.

Juliane held her breath while she watched the

exchange. Would Nathan be able to convince Lukas that he shouldn't drive himself home? Thankfully, Lukas was a happy drunk, not a surly one.

"Then how do you expect me to get home?" Lukas slurred through his question.

"Juliane will drive you." Nathan turned her way.

Her heart sank into her stomach. "Me?"

"Yes." Nathan pulled her aside for a moment. "You can drive him to his apartment. Unlock his door, then keep his keys, so he won't decide to drive himself out for a White Castle. I'd do it myself, but I have to help load all the tables and stuff we borrowed, so the guys can return them."

"I don't know where he lives."

"In that complex a couple of blocks from campus. You know the one I mean?"

Juliane nodded.

"Good. I'll be there in a few minutes to pick you up. Think of this as your good deed for the day."

Letting out her breath, Juliane glanced at Lukas, who stumbled toward them. He was still grinning, his eyes glazed over as he stopped beside her. Taking him home wasn't what she wanted to do, but she couldn't let him drive. "Looks like I'm elected to take you home."

"The pretty lady wants to drive me home?"

Not really. "Sure, get in."

Without an argument, Lukas slumped into the passenger seat. Thankfully, she was able to make the trip without having to stop for a traffic light. Turning into the parking lot, she glanced at Lukas, who was still slumped in his seat. "Which building is yours?"

"This first one." Looking at her, he gave her that silly grin again. "You know…you're pretty. Why haven't I seen you before?"

She ignored the question as she got out. "We need to get you inside. Can you walk?"

"Of course, I can walk." He opened the door and exited the car. He lurched forward but managed not to fall down. "See?"

Once inside the building, Juliane followed Lukas up the stairs to his apartment. She unlocked the door and let it swing open. She turned and looked at him. "You're home. I'm keeping your keys, and Nathan will see that you get them back tomorrow."

He stumbled into the apartment and pulled her with him. "Okay, pretty lady, what do you have for me?"

"Nothing." Her heart hammered as she tried to pull her arm from his grasp.

He gave her that sappy smile, only this time it seemed more like a leer. "You didn't drive me home for nothing."

"I've got to go. Nathan is waiting for me."

"He can just keep waiting." Lukas kicked the door closed, pulled her into his arms and kissed her.

Juliane tried not to panic as she twisted her head

away and kneed him in the groin. He let go of her and slumped over. Seeing her chance to escape, she opened the door and fled down the stairs.

Through the open door, he yelled, "Hey, whad ya do that for? I was only trying to get a kiss."

Maybe that was all he had been trying to do, but she wasn't sticking around to find out. He had scared her. Feeling sick to her stomach, she raced across the parking lot. When Nathan finally picked her up, he asked why she was waiting out in the cold. She told him she hadn't felt like spending time with a drunk. She never told him anything else. She never told anyone about it.

Lukas had done nothing more than kiss her, but she couldn't forget the way he'd scared her with that stolen kiss. Hoping never to see him again, she hadn't gone back to the theater group.

Even with all the time that had passed, the memory still made her shiver. Was Lukas still that kind of man? Maybe not. The Lukas she'd known in college wouldn't have darkened the door of a church. Did his presence here mean he'd changed his lifestyle? She should be glad if that was the case, but his sudden appearance had unnerved her. Thankfully, a great deal of attention wasn't required tonight.

As soon as the rehearsal was over, Juliane rushed over to Tom. "Do you have a few minutes to talk in private?"

Tom wrinkled his brow and shrugged. "Sure, if you want to wait until everyone else has left."

"I'll wait." Juliane left the stage and breathed a sigh of relief when she saw Lukas hurry off in the opposite direction. As she started to sit on the nearby pew, she heard Val call her name and turned. "Did you want me?"

"Yeah. We're all headed to the coffee shop. Are you going to join us?" Her cousin gestured to the group gathered near the door.

Juliane was relieved to see that Lukas wasn't among them. "Sure. I'll be over after I talk to Pastor Tom."

"Okay. We'll see you in a little while." Val hurried down the aisle.

After Val left, Juliane sat on the front pew and tried to study her lines and music while she waited for Pastor Tom. He was having tryouts for small solo parts. She wondered whether Lukas had tried out. When had he done that? When had he moved to town? Had he been in church on recent Sundays? She hadn't seen him. It seemed as though he had appeared out of nowhere.

Juliane shook her head in an attempt to focus on her part instead of letting her thoughts drift back to Lukas. He wasn't even here, and yet he filled her mind. Maybe the initial shock of seeing him again would wear off and she wouldn't think about him anymore. *Wishful thinking.*

"Are you ready to talk?"

Startled, Juliane glanced up to find Pastor Tom standing in front of her. "Oh, sure."

"What do you want to discuss?" Tom sat next to her.

She stared at him for a moment. How was she going to ask her question without seeming ungracious toward Lukas? She should've figured that out while she sat here. She took a deep breath. "Well…I thought Nathan was going to be David. You know Nathan and I were the lead soloists in the Christmas program just a few weeks ago, so I thought we were going to do the leads in this program, as well. I was really surprised to hear that Lukas will be playing that part."

"I know you expected Nathan to be the male lead. He intended to do that, but while you were away on your buying trip this past week, he told me he'd rather not have a lead part since he's going to be extra busy at the bank. Then Lukas showed up at church two weeks ago and volunteered. He has a great voice." Tom wrinkled his brow. "Do you have a problem with that?"

Yeah, but there was no way she could tell Tom about it. "I was concerned that Nathan would be upset."

"I'm glad I could ease your concern." Tom patted her on the shoulder. "I heard Val invite you to join the others at the coffee shop. So I'll let you run along."

"Okay. Thanks for explaining. See you later."

Juliane shuffled down the aisle and contemplated the fact that Lukas had been here for two weeks. She'd been out of town last Sunday, but why hadn't she noticed him the Sunday before? How was it possible to be in the same room as Lukas and not notice him? His good looks and magnetic smile had always drawn attention.

She gave herself a mental scolding. Lukas's attractiveness wasn't the issue. The issue was whether he could be trusted. Their parts in the program meant weeks of interaction. There was no getting around it. Trying to avoid him would be impossible at church as well as in this little town. Would she feel uncomfortable around him? He didn't seem to remember what he'd done. It had been a long time since then. Maybe he truly had changed.

Juliane shrugged into her coat and rushed to her car in the church parking lot. The January night air made her shiver as she brushed snow from her windshield. While she drove the short distance to the coffee shop on Main Street, she hoped she could relax and forget any future dealings with Lukas at least for tonight.

She needed some downtime after her hectic day at the department store that her family owned. Although she loved her father, sometimes working with him was not the easiest. Their ideas about how to run the business often clashed. Things were better now that he was sober—six months and counting—but how long would that last? She'd seen him fall off the wagon often enough to learn her lesson. She could never trust a drinker, not even her father—and especially not Lukas Frey.

Chapter Two

Music, conversation and laughter floated around Lukas while he sat at a table toward the front of the coffee shop. On the small nearby stage, a lone guitarist entertained the crowd while they lingered over their coffee.

Val and Eric Hughes sat across the table from him. This young couple had gone out of their way to make him feel welcome at church from the moment he'd set foot inside the door. In fact, everyone he'd met so far had welcomed him and treated him kindly. More than anything, he wanted their friendship and respect, but would his bad behavior in grad school ruin his chance?

What would happen when Juliane told them about his past? She remembered him from his college years. He feared she was already giving Pastor Tom an earful as she stayed behind to talk to him.

Lukas had heard Val invite Juliane to come, and

he hoped that during this time together he could befriend her. Then maybe she wouldn't have any reason to bring up his past, but that was probably wishful thinking.

"So what do you think?" Eric gestured around the room. "Do we do things up right here in Kellersburg?"

Nodding, Lukas smiled. "It's great to have entertainment on a weeknight."

"You should hear the jazz combo that plays on the weekends." Val looked at him over her coffee cup. "Not bad for a one-horse town."

"Hey, we're at least a two-horse town." Eric chuckled.

"A two-horse town where everyone knows everyone, and at least a quarter of us are related to each other." Val glanced at Carrie Wilson, who sat next to her. "Sometimes that's nice, and other times it can be a pain, right, Carrie?"

"Yeah, it's a real pain being related to you." Laughing, Carrie nodded. "Val's my cousin. So is Juliane."

"Did all of you grow up here?"

"Eric, Carrie, Juliane and I did." Val tapped Adam, Carrie's husband, on the arm. "But Adam here had the good fortune of finding us through Carrie."

"It's a great little town even though you have to put up with the Kellers and their relatives on every corner." Adam winked at his wife.

Lukas took in the good-natured kidding. "Is that why the town's called Kellersburg?"

Eric nodded. "Val's great-great-great-great—"

"Quit enumerating the greats," Val interrupted.

"Okay." Eric laughed. "The town was founded by her ancestors who led a group of settlers from North Carolina to this area."

"Do you get many transplants to your town?" Lukas wondered how he would be accepted. Sometimes people in small towns didn't readily welcome newcomers.

"More these days than when we were kids. The town's been growing a lot in recent years. Kellersburg has always been a wonderful place to raise a family." Grinning, Adam patted his wife's very pregnant figure. "And we're adding to the population."

After taking a gulp of his coffee, Eric glanced at Lukas. "Did I hear Juliane say she knew you in college?"

"Yeah, but not that well. We worked on a theater production at the same time, but we didn't run in the same circles." That was an understatement, and Lukas hoped this conversation wouldn't lead to a discussion of that time.

Thankfully, Juliane wasn't here now, but what would happen when she joined them? What stories would she tell? He barely remembered her, had no idea what she'd seen him do. So many of his memories from that period were a blur. How else could he explain meeting such a beautiful woman and forgetting her almost completely?

He glanced toward the door to see whether she'd arrived. Although he was worried about facing her, part of him hoped he could show her that he wasn't the same Lukas Frey she'd seen all those years ago. The other part feared what she might reveal.

Lukas couldn't forget the way the color had drained from her face when he'd told her he had the male lead in the musical. He wasn't sure whether the look in her caramel-colored eyes tonight had been disgust or pity. Either way, he wanted to change her opinion of him.

"There's Juliane." Val waved her hand above her head. "Juliane, we're over here."

Lukas watched as she made her way toward them. Was he imagining the displeasure in her expression, or was he being paranoid about the past? He jumped up and pulled out the empty chair next to him. "Glad you could make it."

Juliane took the chair he offered. "My meeting with Pastor Tom didn't take long."

"That's good," Val said before Lukas could add anything.

As the waitress came to take Juliane's order, he realized that she hadn't hesitated to sit beside him. Maybe he was mistaken about her expression when she'd entered the coffee shop. The vanilla scent of her perfume mingled with the smell of brewing coffee. He took in the chin-length, light brown hair that framed her pretty face and matched her eyes and wondered why he was aware of so many details about her.

After the waitress left, Juliane took off her coat and let it hang over the back of her chair. "I see you've found our favorite hangout."

"Yeah, thanks to Val and Eric."

Was she uneasy about his presence here, or was she just making conversation? Why was he always second-guessing himself? She'd been very polite, but her politeness seemed forced. Or was he projecting his own discomfort onto her? He had to get a grip and quit imagining that her expression was filled with disgust when she looked his way.

A few minutes later, the waitress deposited a steaming cup of coffee in front of Juliane. Val and Carrie began peppering Juliane with questions about how she knew Lukas. She fidgeted in her chair and gave him a tentative smile. What was she going to say? His stomach knotted as he waited for her answer.

She shook her head. "We barely knew each other. During my freshman year, we were in a couple of musicals together, but Lukas was one of the leads, and I was only in the chorus. We didn't have much interaction, did we, Lukas?"

"That's right." Lukas breathed a sigh of relief. She didn't want to discuss the past any more than he did.

"When did you move to Kellersburg?" she asked, as if she was eager to change the subject.

"A couple of weeks ago. I actually started my new job over a month ago, but I was driving back and forth between here and Cincinnati for a couple of weeks until I found a house I wanted to buy."

"So are you all settled?" Juliane stirred her coffee, then took a sip.

"I haven't hung any pictures, if that's what you mean."

Leaning forward, Carrie tapped Lukas on the arm. "You should have Juliane help you decorate. She's great at that."

Juliane eyed her cousin with unmistakable irritation. "Don't volunteer me for anything. I have enough work to do."

Carrie held up a hand. "I was only making a suggestion."

Juliane sighed. "Sorry. That's okay. I'm just feeling the pressure of running the store. You know after the first of the year we have to do inventory. That means a lot of extra work."

Lukas surreptitiously watched Juliane as she continued to run new store promotions by her cousins to get their input. Was the fact that she was eye-catching with her feminine curves the reason he had a vague memory of her from his graduate school years? Even though he couldn't place their exact meeting, she'd obviously made something of an impression on him. Yet uneasiness about her that he couldn't quite grasp floated at the back of his mind.

Even though men turned to look when she walked into a room, something more than her good looks sparked his interest. Still, he knew he had to keep any attraction to her in check. He wanted her friendship. He had little doubt that she'd never be interested in anything more because of his past.

"You'd like to do that, wouldn't you, Lukas?"

Lukas glanced at Val and tried to hide the fact that he hadn't been listening and had no idea what she was talking about. "I'm not sure."

"Let me convince you."

"Okay." He hoped his noncommittal response would somehow get her to give him another clue about her question.

"I know you just moved here, but it would be a good way to meet a lot of people in the congregation."

"Yeah, everyone has a great time at the Valentine's banquet." Eric clapped Lukas on the back.

"Tell me what's involved." Lukas hoped his inquiry wouldn't signal his inattention to their conversation.

"Sure." Val glanced around the table. "We're all involved in some way. I'm responsible for providing the food and getting the youth group to help serve it.

Carrie and Adam are heading the committee in charge of decorating the fellowship hall. Eric is helping with the setup. Juliane, as I mentioned, is in charge of entertainment. And I thought since the two of you have worked together before that you'd be able to help her out."

Val had dropped another opportunity to get involved in the community in his lap—just what he wanted. Dealing with Juliane was a bonus. Maybe this would be his chance to have her get to know the new him.

Lukas turned to look at her. The color had drained from her face again. She didn't want to work with him. Had anyone else noticed? Did he dare say yes and put her on the spot? "What do you say, Juliane?"

Lukas's question rattled around in Juliane's brain and created the beginnings of a headache. She clenched and unclenched her fist in her lap. Eager faces around the table told her she had to say yes.

What was God trying to teach her by dropping Lukas into her life on top of the other challenges she faced?

Juliane nodded and tried to smile. Smiling had certainly been difficult tonight. "I'm sure between the two of us we can come up with some super entertainment."

"Great. When do we start?" Lukas leaned forward with enthusiasm, but he seemed surprised by her agreement.

Juliane shrugged. "Whenever you want."

What was his motivation? Why had he involved himself in church as soon as he moved here?

"When are you free to discuss it?"

A sinking sensation hit her stomach. Free to discuss it—as in meeting with him one-on-one? Yeah. That was probably what he meant. Taking a deep breath, she pulled her BlackBerry out of her purse and wished her calendar were full for the foreseeable future. "I'll have to check."

"Great." He reached into a pocket in his coat and brought out his BlackBerry, too.

Breaking eye contact, she searched her calendar. "I have a couple of free evenings, but since I just returned from a business trip, I have to check with my dad to make sure he hasn't planned a store meeting I don't know about yet."

"That's fine." He narrowed his gaze. "Is Raymond Keller your dad?"

"Yes, why?" Juliane's heart jumped into her throat. How could Lukas possibly know her dad?

"I met him the other day at the chamber of commerce meeting. I'm just now making the connection. Your dad's quite the storyteller."

"Yeah, he does enjoy a good laugh." Juliane couldn't help comparing the two men—both charming but flawed.

"He said I should meet you when you got back from your buying trip."

Juliane wondered what had prompted her dad to mention her to Lukas. She'd never been the daughter her father wanted to show off—that was her sister, Elise.

He handed her a business card. "Here's my contact information. You can call me after you talk with your dad."

"Thanks." She took it. Her pulse quickened as their fingers touched. Her reaction caught her off guard. She'd let his charm undermine her initial caution. Nothing seemed right since Lukas had shown up. She shoved the card into her purse and hoped that when she looked up Lukas wouldn't be staring at her.

She got her wish. He was already deep in conversation with Adam and Eric as they discussed the local high school basketball team. So why was she disappointed that he wasn't paying any attention to her?

His sudden reappearance had thrown her completely off balance, but she wasn't going to let that continue.

She gave herself a mental pep talk. *Forget Lukas Frey.* But how could she when she had to interact with him on a weekly basis, if not more? Well, she was no wimp. She would deal with it one way or another. She wouldn't think about herself anymore.

Juliane turned to Val. "Is your mom watching the kids?"

"Yeah. She calls these nights her grandma duty, but she loves it." Val took a sip of her coffee.

Carrie patted her very protruding stomach. "My mom can hardly wait for her grandma duty."

Carrie and Val laughed, and Juliane joined them. Her mother was just hoping she'd get to be a grandma one day. But Juliane had no potential marriage partners. The few eligible men in town held little interest for her.

Except Lukas Frey. She shook away the thought. After the way he'd behaved all those years ago, how could that thought have popped into her head? Lukas Frey should be the last man on her list of marriage prospects. Romantic ideas about him had no place in her thinking. No matter how attractive he was, she knew better than to think of him that way. She knew all too well what marriage with an alcoholic was like.

Never. That wouldn't happen to her.

Juliane cast a furtive glance in Lukas's direction. He drained the last of his coffee while he listened to Eric's assessment of the Cincinnati Bengals football team and the upcoming NFL playoff games. Looking away, she felt oddly out of place. She didn't fit in with the guys discussing sports or the women talking about babies.

Sometimes being single was tough. Everything around her seemed geared for couples, especially at church. She glanced at Lukas again. Did single guys ever feel out of place in a couples' world, or was that only a malady of single women?

"Did I hear that Elise is coming home?" Val asked before Juliane could answer her own question.

"Yeah, she's flying into Cincinnati two weeks from Sunday. Mom and Dad are so excited that she's finally decided to quit roaming the high seas." Juliane thought of her sister, who had worked for a cruise line as an entertainer for the past six years.

Juliane had to admit that she was sometimes jealous of her sister. Elise had had the courage to go against their parents' wishes and drop out of college and see the world, while Juliane had returned to her hometown after college to a mundane life. She shouldn't begrudge her sister the opportunity she'd taken to use her singing talent to earn a living.

Still, Juliane often wondered what turns her life might have taken if she'd pursued a career using her musical talents as her sister had. But there was no going back. Being the oldest child, Juliane had felt the responsibility of helping with the family business. Elise had always been the outgoing adventurous one, anyway. It was part of her charm. A charm Juliane had always known she lacked.

"So what brings Elise home?" Carrie asked.

Shrugging, Juliane shook her head. "I'm not sure. She just called a few weeks ago and said she wasn't signing a new contract with the cruise line and would be coming home as soon as her current contract is finished. No other explanation."

Val laid a hand on one of Juliane's arms. "Maybe she's tired of living on a cruise ship."

Juliane nodded. "Probably. She's moving in with me."

"That's great." Val sat forward in her seat. "She'll also be a great addition to the choir."

"She certainly will." Juliane couldn't help thinking that if Elise had returned sooner, she might have gotten Juliane's part in the Winter Festival program. But wasn't that what she'd wished for earlier—to let someone else have the part so she wouldn't have to deal with Lukas? Elise could fill that role with ease, but deep inside, Juliane didn't want to relinquish it to her sister.

Elise, two years Juliane's junior, had more singing talent. Elise was also the pretty sister, who had attracted boys at every turn while they were growing up. Even the boy Juliane had longed to date in high school had fallen for Elise instead. Despite being older, Juliane felt as though she couldn't compete with her sister on any front. How would her return affect Juliane's life?

"I'm so glad she's coming home." Carrie clapped her hands. "It'll be like old times—the four of us together."

Shaking her head, Juliane laughed. "I kind of doubt it'll be like old times with you about to give birth and Val with two kids already."

Carrie sighed. "Well, maybe not old times, but it'll still be fun to have a girls' night out or spend a Saturday shopping in Cincinnati."

"Did I hear you say something about shopping?" Adam leaned closer to Carrie. "Haven't you had enough shopping trips to Cincinnati lately?"

Carrie gave Adam a playful swat. "We're talking about when Elise gets home."

"So now you're going to use Elise's return as an excuse to go shopping." Adam tried to act displeased as he gazed adoringly at his wife.

"You know we still need things for the baby."

Eric clapped Adam on the back. "Hey, pal, haven't you learned by now that there are always at least a hundred reasons to go shopping?"

"Yeah, what was I thinking?" Adam batted himself on the side of his head.

Eric stood and pushed his chair under the table. "Well, gang, it's been fun, but I believe about now Val's mom has had enough of our kids, but she won't ever say so."

"Or maybe you're worried that she's spoiled them rotten while we've been gone." Chuckling, Val slipped an arm through her husband's.

Juliane smiled at the jovial exchange, but her thoughts were still caught on what life would be like with her sister back home. She wanted to be as excited as her cousins, but ever since she'd learned of Elise's plans, she worried that she'd fall into her sister's shadow again.

The troubling thoughts weighed heavily on Juliane's mind as she shrugged into her coat and slung her purse strap over her shoulder. Juliane loved her sister, but she wasn't sure how things would play out with Elise. She shouldn't be envious of her sister. But she couldn't shake the unkind thoughts. How could she be right with God when she harbored jealousy in her heart?

Now Juliane not only had to deal with her feelings about Elise, but Lukas, too. The perfect storm of events was bearing down on her life.

Lukas hurried after Juliane. As she was about to open the coffee shop door, he reached around and opened it for her. "Let me walk you to your car."

She stopped abruptly in the doorway and looked up at him. "Thanks, but I'm only parked a few steps down the block."

He didn't miss the surprise brimming in her eyes. "Then it won't be much trouble to escort you."

"Okay, if that's what you want." Despite the wary set to her shoulders and the resignation in her voice, she smiled and plucked her keys from her purse.

Wondering what thoughts lay behind the smile, Lukas fell into step beside her. Was she uncomfortable in his presence? He'd asked himself that question at least a dozen times tonight since their initial meeting.

Her hurried pace made her heels click against the concrete sidewalk. In the crisp cold air, the sound echoed off the nearby buildings and into the darkness. Was she in a rush to get away from him? Probably. He wished he were brave enough to ask.

More questions formed in his mind. He wanted to know what she'd told Pastor Tom, but this wasn't the time or place to ask her. Still, the question sat on the tip of his tongue. He gritted his teeth in order not to let it slip out.

A few yards down the street, she stopped beside a dark blue subcompact, a patch of unmelted snow still sitting on the back bumper. "Well, this is it. Thanks for walking me to my car, but it really wasn't necessary."

"I wanted to, so we could set a tentative time to meet. Then you can check with your dad before you confirm it."

"I guess." Even in the dim light, he detected the uneasiness in her expression as she glanced his way. "When did you have in mind?"

"How about dinner on Friday night?"

"Dinner?"

"Yeah."

She shook her head. "A dinner meeting isn't possible."

"Why not? We both have to eat."

"I work the concession stand at the high school basketball games on Friday nights when they have a home game. And this Friday is a home game."

"How about letting me work the concession stand with you? If it's anything like my high school years, the boosters are always looking for more help. We can talk afterward."

Juliane shrugged. "Let me check first."

"Should I call you, or do you want to call me?"

"I'll call you." She hurriedly got into her car and closed the door, not waiting for him to respond.

Feeling shut out, he stood at the curb and shoved his hands into his coat pockets. The car lights came on, the engine roared to life and she drove away. He watched as her car made the turn at the town square and disappeared.

"She's often in a hurry. Sometimes, I wish she'd slow down and enjoy life. She's too driven."

Lukas turned at the sound of the female voice. Val stood a few feet away. He took a step toward her. "So I see."

"Eric got waylaid. He ran into a guy from work as we were leaving." Val looked back at the coffee shop, then returned her gaze to Lukas. "I hope you didn't mind that I asked you to work with Juliane on the banquet. I realized later that you might think I was a little pushy."

Lukas chuckled. "No problem. I'm glad to get involved."

"Then you don't mind working with Juliane?"

"No. Why?"

Shrugging, Val let her gaze slide away and grimaced. "I noticed after I made the suggestion that there was some hesitation, especially from Juliane."

"Then…shouldn't you be asking her the questions?"

"Probably, but I thought you might know why she hesitated. Do you?"

Talk about being put on the spot. Christians were supposed to tell the truth, but that was the last thing Lukas wanted to do right now. The temptation to lie lurked in his mind. Could he give Val a reason without going into detail?

Lukas took a deep breath and let it out slowly. "I have an idea."

"And what's that?"

"Um…" He couldn't believe he had to explain things already. He thought he'd have a chance for people to get to know him—the new man in Christ— first, before he had to tell them about the old one. "Probably because I lived on the wild side when Juliane knew me during college. I'm sure it was a shock for her to see me in church."

"Oh." Val just stared at him.

Now what did he say? What was she thinking? What would these people say when they found out the details of his past? He doubted Juliane would keep it from them. Before he could say more, Eric strode toward them.

He put an arm around Val's shoulders, his breath visible in the cold air. "Sorry about that, hon. We'd better get home."

Val smiled at her husband. "Sure." Then she turned to Lukas. "See you in church on Sunday."

"I'll be there." Lukas started toward his car.

Just ahead of him, Val and Eric walked arm in arm. While he watched them, loneliness crept into his soul. Would he ever find a love like theirs? What kind of a woman would be willing to take a chance on him, a man who was trying to live down his past?

The clock on the top of the courthouse in the square began to chime. He looked up. The clock's illuminated face read ten o'clock. It was past time to check on his grandfather.

As Lukas drove along the quiet streets, he replayed the evening in his mind. What pushed him to seek out Juliane when she could bring him down with a word or two? He tried to convince himself that he only wanted to show her how he'd changed, but he couldn't deny his attraction to her.

Although his ulterior motive to get her on his side didn't give him a good feeling, he still wanted to cultivate her friendship. Was there any chance she'd accept his friendship? He wished he could remember what he'd done to make her so wary of him. Of course, there was every chance he'd be finding out soon. Val would surely ask Juliane about his past, and the whole mess of his life would come out in that conversation. He might as well accept the inevitable.

Was it God's plan that everyone should know about his former behavior? Maybe that was the way it was supposed to work. Like that scripture about carrying each other's burdens. Christians were supposed to help each other, but Lukas still had trouble trusting people to do that.

Stopping his car in his grandfather's driveway, Lukas noticed that his grandfather had shoveled the snow from the drive and the sidewalks. The man was going to kill himself with overwork. Lights shone through the window in the front room. As he approached the porch, he could hear the TV. Grandpa was watching TV again with the volume turned on high. He slipped the key into the lock and opened the door.

Lukas glanced around as he entered the living room. His grandfather lay sleeping in his recliner while the TV blared at a deafening decibel. Lukas walked across the room, grabbed the remote and shut off the TV.

As soon as the screen went blank, his grandfather sat straight up and waved a hand at Lukas. "Why did you turn that off? I was watching my program."

Lukas tried not to laugh as he raised his voice so his grandfather could hear. "Grandpa, you were sleeping."

"I just had my eyes closed," his grandfather said, his heavy German accent obvious.

"Okay, whatever you say."

"Why are you here?"

"Just stopping by to see how you're doing."

"I am fine. See?" Ferdinand held his hands out in front of him. "Turn the TV back on, and let me watch my show."

Lukas braced himself as he punched the remote. When the TV blared back to life, he quickly lowered the volume.

"Turn that back up."

Pressing the pause button on the remote for the digital recorder, Lukas turned to his grandfather. "I've paused your show, and you can watch this with the volume as loud as you want after I leave."

"You can do that anytime." The older man scowled. "I didn't ask you to come here. I was getting along fine until you came to town. Now you are in my face all the time."

Taking a deep breath, Lukas bit back a nasty retort. He understood that his grandfather didn't like feeling as though he needed to have someone to watch after him. He was a proud, brave man, who had risked his life to find freedom on the other side of the Berlin Wall. Lukas had taken too long to realize what his grandfather had done and to appreciate the courage he'd needed in his escape from East Berlin and communism.

"I know you didn't, but I love you, Grandpa. This is a chance for us to be close again. Now that I've turned my life around."

Ferd pushed himself out of the recliner. "Yes, and I am glad for that. But that doesn't mean you need to take care of me. I can take care of myself. Make my own decisions. Watch my programs as loud as I like."

"We can get you fitted for hearing aids."

"Why do I need hearing aids, if I can turn up the volume?"

"Then I won't have to shout or repeat myself when we talk." Lukas laid a hand on his grandfather's shoulder. "It wouldn't be so bad to give them a try. What do you say?"

Letting out a long sigh, Ferdinand gave Lukas a resigned nod. "I suppose you are right. I will try them just for you."

"Thank you, Grandpa. I'll arrange an appointment for you." Lukas handed the remote to his grandfather. "Now I'll head home, and you can watch your show."

"Don't forget I go to the senior center on Monday, Wednesday and Friday mornings, so don't make an appointment that interferes."

"I'll try to avoid those times." Lukas walked to the door, then turned back to his grandfather. "Is there anything you need?"

"No, I am fine."

"Okay, see you tomorrow."

Before Lukas shut the door behind him, the TV blared again. He almost expected the windows to shatter from the volume. As he drove the short block to his own house, he wondered whether he'd be able to get his grandfather to use the hearing aids even if he got them.

After entering his house, Lukas went into the small bedroom that served as his office. He plunked his briefcase onto the desk and noticed the blinking red light on the answering machine. Grabbing a pen and paper, he hit the play button.

Juliane's voice floated through the room. "Lukas, this is Juliane Keller. I spoke with the woman in charge of the concession booth, and she said she'd love to have more help. So I guess we're on for Friday night. You can call me for details."

As Juliane recited her phone number, he scribbled it on the notepad. Dropping into the nearby chair, he stared at the machine. Then he listened to the message a second time to make sure he hadn't imagined the whole thing. After the way she'd rushed off tonight, he never expected to hear from her so soon, if at all.

Leaning back, he laced his fingers behind his head and smiled. Maybe this wasn't going to turn out badly, after all. But he cautioned himself not to get too carried away just because Juliane had agreed to meet with him.

Taking one day at a time made his life easier. He reminded himself not to borrow trouble from tomorrow, because God was always there to help today.

Chapter Three

The roar of the crowd filtered through the hallway of the gymnasium, while the high school band played the team fight song. Juliane knew from experience that this signaled the entrance of the Kellersburg Tigers onto the basketball court. Bustling around the concession stand, the members of the basketball boosters prepared and sold hot dogs, nachos, popcorn and various other snacks and soft drinks.

While Juliane helped Carol Donovan prepare for the halftime onslaught of fans, she wondered where Lukas was. She'd told him to be here at six-thirty, but it was nearly seven, and he hadn't arrived. Telling herself she might as well get the meeting with Lukas over, she'd given herself a pep talk about tonight. Now, if he didn't show, she'd have to do it all over again.

After she'd made arrangements for him to help, she hoped Lukas wouldn't arrive inebriated, or not at all. Or was he like her father—able to function most of the time despite his drinking? After all, Lukas had been falling-down drunk the last time she'd seen him eleven years ago, but maybe he'd gotten more discreet over the years.

She should try to make the best of the whole situation with Lukas. She had to face facts. He was going to be around for the foreseeable future, and she was going to have to learn to live with his presence in town and at church—like it or not.

Still, how was she going to explain, if he didn't show? She didn't want to make excuses for him. Juliane couldn't help thinking about the times she and her mother had stepped in and saved her father from showing up drunk at an event. Through the years she'd given her mother moral support while she dealt with her husband's drinking. How often had Juliane taken his place at functions, always making some excuse for him? She didn't intend to do that for Lukas.

Although family and close friends had witnessed her father's overindulgence, she wondered whether she and her mother had successfully covered for him with other people. Or had they guessed over the years that her father had a drinking problem? She'd never heard any gossip in that regard, but maybe people were careful to avoid letting her hear the unkind talk.

"Juliane, sorry to be so late. I thought I'd never get here." Lukas's voice startled her from her thoughts.

Trying to pretend she wasn't bothered by his late appearance, she turned and smiled. "Oh, that's okay. We've been doing fine without you."

His head lowered, an older man with thinning gray hair stepped from behind Lukas. "It's my fault, miss."

Juliane peered at him. Somehow he looked familiar, but she couldn't pinpoint why. Then he looked up. "Ferd, what are you doing here with Lukas?"

"Juliane!" Ferd smiled.

Stepping closer to her, Lukas knit his eyebrows in a frown. "You know my grandfather?"

"Ferd is your grandfather?"

Lukas nodded. "You asked about him at choir practice, and I told you my grandfather is Ferdinand Engel. Did you forget?"

"No." Juliane glanced from Lukas to his grandfather, then back at Lukas. Although Ferd was much shorter than Lukas, they shared the same startling blue eyes. "I know your grandfather from the senior center, but only as Ferd, not Ferdinand. I volunteer there one morning a week."

"You don't have to talk about me like I'm not here," Ferd said.

"Sorry." Juliane hugged the older man. "I'm so surprised to see you here. I didn't recognize you at first."

"And I did not realize when Lukas told me he was meeting a woman from church that he was meeting Juliane from the senior center. I was expecting someone much older and not so pretty." Ferd winked and made a sweeping motion with his hand. "I'm here to help, too."

Lukas laid a hand on Ferd's shoulder. "Grandpa, I didn't say you were here to help."

Shaking his head, Ferd wagged a finger at Lukas, then turned to Juliane. "He thinks he has to babysit me."

Juliane didn't miss the look of exasperation on Lukas's face. "We can always use another hand, especially at halftime."

Ferd grinned at Lukas. "See. I told you so. Just because you think I'm a useless old man. Juliane knows I'm a big help at the senior center."

Pressing his lips together in a grim line, Lukas looked as though he was forcing himself to say nothing. Juliane could only guess what might be going through his mind. Did she dare offer an opinion in this family dispute? Probably not, but she could turn the discussion in another direction. She couldn't believe she was actually trying to help Lukas. "Let me make some introductions."

Lukas's expression appeared to change from exasperation to relief. "Sure."

First, Juliane introduced them to Carol Donovan, then to the rest of the crew. Carol immediately gave Ferd a job filling bags with popcorn. She asked Lukas to help Juliane cover the drink station.

After Ferd started his task, Juliane checked to

make sure there was a good supply of cups near the soft drink fountain. She hoped she hadn't made a mistake by inviting Lukas to join the boosters.

As she worked, Lukas came up beside her. "Is there anything specific you'd like me to do?"

"Take drink orders. These are for fountain drinks." She held up a large plastic cup, trying to ignore the way his nearness made her pulse quicken. This close, she could tell that there was no trace of alcohol on his breath. Had he really changed? It was too soon to tell. Still trying to get a grip on her emotions, she picked up a foam cup. "These are for the hot drinks that are over here."

Lukas followed her to the back of the concession stand to a table where two large urns sat—one labeled Coffee and the other Hot Chocolate. "Looks like everything's in order."

"It's pretty easy. We've been doing this for years. We have a lull now, but starting just before the end of the first quarter, we get a steady stream of customers. Then it gets a little crazy at halftime."

As a roar went up from the crowd, Lukas leaned closer to her and whispered, "Thanks for helping me with my grandfather."

"Glad to help. Your grandfather is a very nice man." She tried not to let his closeness affect her, but he set her emotions on edge. She didn't want to think for one instant that her reaction had anything to do with a romantic interest in the man. She'd spent nearly her whole life helping her mom deal with her father's drinking. How could she possibly entertain a fascination with a man who had the same problem?

"Yeah, but he can be stubborn sometimes."

"Can't we all?"

"I guess." Lukas chuckled. "I didn't plan to have him come with me until I stopped by his house on my way home from work. He was down in his basement and could barely make it up the stairs. He couldn't get his breath, so I was afraid to leave him alone."

"You were smart to bring him." Juliane's opinion of Lukas rose a notch. He really cared about his grandfather.

"He doesn't like to admit he needs help."

"Lots of people are like that." Juliane couldn't help thinking of her father. Maybe Lukas, too. But she had to admit that so far he showed no signs of his wild past.

Before either of them could make another comment, a group of folks approached the concession stand, and time for conversation ceased. But questions about Lukas popped in her mind like the popping kernels in the nearby popcorn machine. Her worry about him showing up drunk had been laid to rest. Was he on the wagon all the time now, or did he have relapses similar to her dad's?

Her dad wouldn't have a drink for months, but

without warning, she would find him at the store passed out, slumped over his desk in his office. Other times she and her mother would discover him passed out in his recliner at home. The images tore at her heart and made her sick to her stomach. She hated dealing with this problem, but she'd learned to live with it.

Time and time again her father broke her heart. She couldn't imagine the anguish that his drinking had caused her mother. Juliane had made a vow that she would never live like her mother—imprisoned by her husband's drinking.

Juliane had prayed for years that God would somehow help her father, but he'd never changed. Sometimes she wanted to blame God, but deep in her heart she knew nothing would change until her father wanted God's help. She couldn't blame God for her father's troubles.

Juliane glanced at Lukas, who laughed and talked with the customers as he waited on them. She had to admit that he had a way with people. She had recognized his ability to relate during choir practice and later at the coffee shop. His outgoing personality probably made him a wonderful plant manager. He knew how to work with and manage people.

The puzzling thoughts continued to plague Juliane while she waited on customers. The squeal of sneakers, the thud of a dribbled basketball on the hardwood and the cheers of the crowd did nothing to lift her spirits even though the hometown team was winning. She couldn't reconcile the Lukas she'd known with the one who looked after his grandfather and who laughed and talked with customers as if he'd been a part of this crew and community for years.

As the end of the game drew near, Juliane started to help Carol with the cleanup. Lukas and the rest of the boosters helped the remaining customers whose ranks had grown slim. Finally, the time came to close the concession stand. The impending meeting with Lukas loomed ahead. Despite her agreement to meet with him and her prayers that she would be able to survive their one-on-one talk without letting old prejudices color her thoughts, she wasn't ready. Could he possibly call off the meeting because of his grandfather?

"Juliane?"

Her stomach lurched at the sound of Lukas's voice. Glad he couldn't read her mind, she forced herself to turn slowly. He stood directly in front of her. "Yes?"

"I'd still like to have our meeting, but I need to take my grandfather home. Let's meet at his house instead of going to the coffee shop, okay?" His blue eyes held a pleading look.

Juliane didn't want the meeting at all, but she was stuck. She'd been stuck from the moment Val had asked the two of them to organize the banquet entertainment. Maybe in one quick meeting they could settle it all. Then she wouldn't have to deal with the confusion he caused her anymore. *Wishful thinking.*

Shaking his head, Lukas motioned toward Ferd. "I know this wasn't part of the plan, but…"

She forced a smile. "That's okay. We might as well get it done."

"Great. He lives on Oak Lane. You know where that is?"

"There aren't too many places in this town that I don't know."

"Good. Here's the address." He handed her a slip of paper.

Taking it, Juliane glanced in Ferd's direction. The feisty older man seemed to have lost all his energy. "We'll be done here in a bit. I'll meet you there."

"Sure." He turned to look at Ferd, who sat on a nearby stool. "I'm going to go ahead and take him home now. I'll see you in a few minutes."

"Okay." Juliane watched Lukas assist his grandfather out of the concession stand. Lukas Frey was making a whole new impression on her. She was almost beginning to like him, and that was way too dangerous.

Driving down Oak Lane, Juliane searched for the address Lukas had given her. She barely touched her foot to the gas pedal as her car crept passed tiny houses with snow-covered lawns. Finally, she saw the numbers on a white bungalow illuminated by the nearby streetlight. Lukas's tan, mid-size sedan sat in the driveway. Even his choice of cars surprised her. She'd expected him to drive a fancy sports car like he'd had in college.

As she exited her car, Lukas flew out the door and charged down the front walk. "Something's terribly wrong with my grandfather. I've called nine-one-one. They'll be here any minute."

Juliane took a shaky breath. "Is there anything I can do?"

"Yes. Please wait out here and watch for the ambulance, so they can find the right house."

"Okay."

Lukas barely waited for her answer before he raced back up the walk. A lump formed in her throat as she watched him take the front steps in one bound. Swallowing the lump, she looked heavenward into the starry night and whispered, "Lord, please help Ferd. You know what he needs."

While Juliane waited for the ambulance, she pulled her BlackBerry from her purse and called her mother. When she answered, Juliane told her about Ferd. "Mom, can you get the church prayer chain started?"

"Absolutely. Call me back when you know more."

"I will." In the distance, sirens wailed. "The ambulance is almost here. I'll talk to you later."

As Juliane ended the call, she saw the flashing red and white lights. Stepping off the curb, she waved her hands above her head. The ambulance slowed and pulled into the driveway behind Lukas's car. With hurried efficiency, the paramedics wheeled a gurney across the snowy yard and into the house. Juliane followed behind them.

The reassuring voices of the paramedics floated from the bedroom down the hall, as she listened from the living room. She wasn't quite sure what to do. Should she leave or stay? She supposed she should at least stick around until she found out how Ferd was doing.

While she stood there, Lukas came into the room. He looked her way, worry coloring his face as he approached. "Thanks for your help."

"What's happening? How is he?"

"They're preparing to take him to the hospital." Lukas ran a hand through his hair.

"Did they say what's wrong?"

Shaking his head, Lukas paced back and forth. "We'll find out once we get there."

"I said a prayer for Ferd and called my mom to start the church prayer chain."

"Thanks." Stopping mid-step, Lukas knit his eyebrows as he looked at her. "I knew something wasn't right, but he wouldn't tell me anything."

Before Juliane could reply, the paramedics pushed the gurney with Ferd aboard toward the front door. Lukas rushed after them, and she followed. She stood on the front walk as the paramedics carefully put the gurney into the back of the ambulance.

After locking the front door, Lukas joined her. "I've got another favor to ask."

"What?"

"I'm going to ride in the ambulance with Grandpa. Would you mind driving my car to the hospital?" He reached into his pants' pocket and pulled out his car keys. He held them out to her.

Déjà vu. Juliane stared at him in the dim light, her pulse pounding all over her body. She pushed the bad memories aside as she took the keys. This was for Ferd. She could do this. "Okay, I'll be glad to help any way I can."

"You're a lifesaver."

"I'll meet you at the hospital."

"Thanks again." He waved, then sprinted to the ambulance and hopped in.

Juliane hustled to Lukas's car, the keys biting into her hand. As she opened the car door, she watched the ambulance drive away, lights blinking and sirens wailing. Her concern for Ferd overrode all her thoughts about Lukas and the past for the moment, but she knew that would change.

Driving through the quiet streets toward the hospital did nothing to calm her mind. By the time she reached the hospital, her stomach was tied in knots and her head throbbed. The ambulance pulled away from the entrance as she parked the car in the nearby lot.

She shivered in the cold night air that reminded her of that night eleven years ago. Her mind fought against the unpleasant memories. She wouldn't think about them, not tonight. She had better things to do than dredge up the past.

Juliane shook the disconcerting thoughts from her mind as she entered the emergency waiting room. The place was filled with people of all ages, most of them looking tired and grim. An antiseptic smell permeated the air while the laugh track from a television sitcom blared over the muted conversation. Lukas sat on one of the molded plastic chairs, his head in his hands. When he glanced up, weariness and worry radiated from his eyes.

"How's Ferd?" she asked, knowing that no matter what had happened in the past, God didn't want her to hold it against Lukas now.

"I'm not sure. They're still examining him." Lukas stood as Juliane drew closer. Her hair gleamed in the light cast from the florescent fixtures. Why was he noticing how great she looked when he should be thinking about his grandfather?

"Did they tell you anything?"

Shaking his head, Lukas sighed. "The doctors are getting him stabilized."

"Here are your keys." She held the key ring on one fingertip of her outstretched hand.

Staring at the keys for a moment, he had the oddest feeling that they had some connection with a set of keys in the past. He gave himself a mental shake to clear his mind of the crazy thought. When he took the keys, the cold metal brought the gravity of his grandfather's situation into full focus. "Thanks for driving. I appreciate your help."

"I'm glad to help Ferd any way I can. He's a dear man."

Lukas noticed she'd said nothing about helping him, only his grandfather. Did she still have an unfavorable view of him based on his past? He wished he could change that, but something told him he'd have a lot of work to do on that account.

He'd been sober for nearly six years, and he thanked God every day for sending Bill Martin into his life to show him God's love and a way out of the bottom of a bottle. Despite his mentor's unconditional acceptance and his assurance that God forgives and Christians would, too, Lukas was never quite sure he believed that Christians would accept his past. Juliane had probably witnessed his drunken state enough times to convince her that he was probably not a very reliable man. Could he convince her otherwise? And why did it seem to matter so much to have her approval and acceptance?

Right now he needed a friend. He wanted her to stay, but that was a lot to ask of her. Did he dare? Looking away, he gathered his courage, then returned his gaze to her. "I hope you don't mind staying for a while. I could use some company."

Silently, she stared at him with those caramel-colored eyes. Was he imagining the panic in them? His heart sank. She wanted to leave. He couldn't blame her. She barely knew him, and what she knew didn't give her a favorable impression.

Then, without warning, she sat on the chair next to the one where he'd been sitting. "Sure. I can keep you company. Hospital waiting rooms can be lonely places."

"Thanks." He tried not to let her see how much her willingness to stay meant to him as he returned to his seat. "If it gets too late, I'll call a cab to take you home."

"No need for that. I can call my mom. She'd be glad to pick me up and take me to get my car." Juliane unzipped her purse and pulled out her BlackBerry. "I'll call and give her an update."

While Juliane talked, Lukas closed his eyes for a moment and said a silent prayer of thanks. God had sent him a friend—a somewhat reluctant one from all appearances, but still someone who was willing to help. And best of all, her presence would help keep him safe from his own bad instincts.

A crisis could trigger the urge to find comfort in a

bottle—something Lukas hadn't felt in a good while, but he knew the danger lurked. He was very aware that the feeling could strike at any time. The Lord knew just what he needed—that extra assistance to escape from temptation.

As Juliane ended her conversation, one of the emergency-room doctors made an appearance. Lukas stood as the doctor approached. "How's my grandfather?"

"We've done our initial evaluation, and we have him stabilized. I'm ordering some more tests to determine his condition."

"What tests?"

"First, we'll do a chest X-ray, then a catheterization to determine whether he has any blockage in his arteries." The doctor motioned toward the exam room. "You can see him for a few minutes before they start."

"Thanks." Lukas turned to Juliane. "Do you want to come?"

"If you think it's okay."

Lukas glanced at the doctor for confirmation, and he nodded before Lukas turned back to Juliane. "I know Grandpa would like to see you."

"Okay."

Lukas let Juliane go ahead of him as they entered the room. His eyes closed, Ferd lay on the hospital bed. "Grandpa, how are you?"

Lukas's stomach sank when his grandfather, who

was hooked up to an IV, oxygen and numerous machines, didn't respond. Lukas moved closer and touched Ferd's arm. He opened his eyes, and Lukas read the uncertainty in them. Ferd grasped Lukas's hand. "What did the doctor say?"

"Didn't he tell you what they are going to do?"

Ferd nodded. "I didn't understand."

"Grandpa, can you hear what the doctor is saying?"

"Some of it."

Lukas sighed, wishing there was something he could do about his grandfather's hearing problem. "Would you like me to tell them that they should talk louder so you can hear them?"

Nodding, Ferd closed his eyes again.

"Are you in pain?"

"No." Ferd's voice sounded barely above a whisper.

"Juliane is here, too. We're praying for you."

Ferd smiled weakly as he looked toward Juliane. "Thank you for coming. You are a wonderful young woman." Ferd turned to Lukas. "You ought to grab this one before she gets away. She would make you a good wife."

Embarrassed by his grandfather's pronouncement, Lukas didn't dare look at Juliane. She was probably thinking he was the last man she wanted for a husband. Did he dare say anything? Probably better to ignore it.

"The doctors are going to take good care of you," he said instead.

Ferd waved a hand at Lukas. "I'm not so sure those doctors know what they're talking about."

"Grandpa, please listen to them. They only want to help you."

Juliane stepped closer to the bed. "Lukas is right, Ferd. The doctors are doing their best to find out what's wrong and help you get better."

Ferd sighed. "I suppose you are right."

A nurse and an orderly came into the room. The nurse's shoes barely made a sound as she walked to the head of the bed. "Okay, young man, we're off to take a picture of your chest."

As the orderly prepared Ferd to go to the radiation department for an X-ray, Lukas took the nurse aside and told her about his grandfather's hearing. She assured Lukas that she would make sure his grandfather understood everything.

After they wheeled Ferd away, Lukas and Juliane returned to the waiting room. Lukas looked over at her. "We could be here for a while. Do you want to see if we can find something to eat or drink?"

"I can look, so you can stay. That way you'll be here when your grandfather returns or if the doctors or nurses need to tell you something."

"Thanks. I appreciate that."

"The cafeteria is closed, but I'm sure I can find a vending machine."

"That'll be fine."

"What would you like?"

"I'll take a cola."

"Any snacks?"

"Whatever." Shrugging, Lukas reached into his pants' pocket, pulled out a money clip and slipped a ten-dollar bill from it. He held it out to Juliane. "This ought to cover it."

She shook her head. "Keep your money. It's my treat."

"Thanks." Lukas watched her disappear down the hall. Despite her helpfulness tonight, he still sensed her unease around him. He laughed a little to himself at the irony. She was probably thinking about how she couldn't wait to leave while he…well, he couldn't seem to help thinking about how much better and easier things seemed to be when he faced them with her by his side.

Chapter Four

Praying for Ferd and herself, Juliane hurried down the hall as she searched for a vending machine. Not sure what she was still doing here, she hoped her prayers might give her an answer. Why had she agreed to stay with Lukas? She had done her good deed in getting his car to the hospital. Ferd was in capable hands now, so Juliane was tempted to call her mother to come and get her, despite her offer to keep Lukas company.

Juliane wished her feelings about Lukas didn't seem so complicated. Maybe she was only making it that way because she couldn't get over the fact that, besides having a handsome face that was hard to overlook, tonight he was a very likable man. His concern for his grandfather affected her in a way she couldn't decipher and made him completely different from the Lukas Frey who used to get drunk—too drunk to remember much about their troublesome encounter all those years ago.

While she let the conflicting emotions roil through her mind, she spotted the vending machines. Trying to push aside all of her contradictory thoughts, she perused the contents of the machines and quickly purchased a couple of colas, two candy bars, a bag of chips and a bag of pretzels. She hoped Lukas wasn't looking for good nutrition.

As she made her way back, she fought against the unpleasant memories about Lukas—the same ones she'd been fighting all evening. This wasn't the time to let old offenses stand in the way of helping someone. Lukas was new to the community and needed a friend. No one else was here to help, so it fell to her to be that friend. And besides, when he'd looked at her with those blue, blue eyes full of anxiety and said he could use some company, she hadn't been able to say no.

When she walked back into the emergency waiting area, Lukas had moved. He was sitting in a chair near the double doors that led to the room where the doctors examined the patients. His head was bowed, and he appeared to be praying. Had he talked to the doctors? Had they given him bad news? She didn't want to disturb him, so she waited quietly nearby.

After a few minutes, he raised his head and glanced her way. "So you found something."

"I did. Some good old-fashioned junk food—perfect late-night emergency-room cuisine." She held up her purchases. "Take your pick."

He stood and walked over to her. Grabbing one of the colas, Lukas chuckled. "My kind of food. We can share the chips and pretzels. I'll let you have first dibs on the candy."

"Okay." Noticing how the waiting area was nearly empty now, Juliane made her way to a chair near the double doors where Lukas had been sitting. She looked over at Lukas as he resumed his seat next to her. "Any more word from the doctors? Is everything okay with your grandfather?"

"No answers yet. I don't know any more than I did before you left."

"Since you moved, I thought maybe—"

"I moved to be closer to the doors in case the doctors want to talk to me."

Leaning back in the chair, Lukas twisted the cap off his cola. "They told me they haven't found anything conclusive. They're running more tests. The nurse said she'd keep me updated."

"I guess that's good." Juliane didn't have a clue as to what else she should say now. Opening the bag of pretzels, she hoped eating would save her from having to make small talk. She popped several pretzels into her mouth as she held the bag out to Lukas.

"Thanks." He dumped some pretzels into his hand

but stopped before he ate them. "I can't thank you enough for staying around. I hope you understand how much I appreciate this."

Juliane didn't know how to respond. Thankfully her mouth was full of pretzels. Nodding, she chewed slowly. Maybe by the time she swallowed, she could come up with a response. She took a swig of cola, then looked his way. "You don't have to thank me. It's nothing."

"But it's something to me."

"I'm glad to help out however I can."

He opened his mouth as if he was going to say something, then closed it. He sat silently for a minute twisting the cap on and off the bottle of cola. After he ate several pretzels, he looked at her again. "Could I clear the air between us?"

"What do you mean?"

"About the past."

Juliane's stomach sank, and her heart raced. Did he suddenly remember the way he'd acted that night? She didn't want to discuss it. She didn't even want to think about it—not that she'd been able to stop herself all evening. She swallowed hard. "What about it?"

He took a deep breath. "I wanted to apologize for anything I may have done to offend you in the past, and to let you know that I've changed."

"I can see that."

"But you're not sure."

He was certainly putting her on the spot. She bit her lower lip. He hadn't said anything about that night. Maybe he still didn't remember. "Am I that transparent?"

He smiled, a hint of relief on his face. "Just a little. From the moment I met you again at choir practice the other night, I sensed that you had some big reservations where I'm concerned."

Juliane knew she had to tell the truth. "Yeah… maybe some."

"That's what I thought." He sighed. "When you told me you remembered me from your college years, I knew I probably wasn't on your list of people who had impressed you—at least in a good way. I'm sure you considered me obnoxious."

"Are you trying to make me say bad things about you?"

His smile turned into a full-fledged laugh. "No, I wanted you to know that I understand if you don't have a very high opinion of me. Did you ever see me sober?"

"Well…when you were performing. I guess."

"That's what I thought." He shook his head, a faraway look in his eyes. "I'm not very proud of that time in my life. I drank too much and studied too little. I'm still amazed that I managed to earn my degrees and find a job."

"What changed your life?"

"First, I got fired from that job I'm surprised I got."

"So that made you mend your ways?"

Lukas laughed halfheartedly. "No, not immediately. Right after I got fired, I went on an extended binge."

"That made you change?" Juliane wondered where this was going.

"Not the binge, but the consequences. I was arrested for drunken driving. I damaged a lot of property—sideswiped a half-dozen parked cars. I'm thankful that I didn't kill anyone."

Juliane munched on some chips as his confession whirled around in her mind. His admission made her think about that night. What would he say if she told him about it? She shook the thought away. This wasn't the time to bring it up. He was trying to make some kind of amends, and bringing up his bad behavior wasn't going to help. "Then what happened?"

"I called my former boss."

"You did? Why?"

"Because when he fired me, he told me he was doing it to wake me up. And if I needed any help, any time, he said I should call him."

Juliane was impressed. If Lukas had been her employee, would she have done the same thing, or would she have washed her hands of him? She was ashamed to admit that the latter was probably more likely. "Why did he do that?"

"Because he saw something in me that I didn't see in myself—potential."

"What do you mean by that?"

"I'm not sure I can explain it exactly." Sighing, Lukas shook his head. "My former boss Bill Martin is a Christian, and he never failed to let me know that God loved me—no matter what I had done. That was his message even when he was firing me."

"Did you believe him?"

"Hardly."

"Then why did you call him when you were arrested?"

"He was the only person I knew that I thought would help me."

"What about your family? Your grandfather?"

"I wasn't close to my family for a long time." Lukas lowered his head and ran a hand through his hair, then shook his head. "Whoa. You don't want to listen to my life's story."

"I'll listen if you want to tell it." Juliane didn't miss the surprise in his expression when he looked her way.

He took a big gulp of his drink, then gave her a crooked smile. "You might have noticed my grandfather's German accent."

"I did. What does that have to do with your relationship with your family?"

"Well…being a dumb kid, I was embarrassed that everyone in my family spoke with heavy accents. I had no idea what it took for them to escape from East Germany and communism."

"Wow! They did that?"

Taking another swig of his cola, Lukas nodded. "See? Everyone who hears that is impressed, but all I could see back then were parents who weren't like everyone else's."

"You were ashamed of them?"

"Yeah. Dumb, wasn't I?"

"Should I agree with you?" Juliane smiled, then bit into another pretzel.

"It doesn't matter whether you say so. I know I was. I was dumb about a lot of things." Lukas continued talking without looking at her, almost as if he were telling the story to the empty chairs across the room. "I was also on the shy side, but when I got my first taste of a beer buzz, I wasn't shy anymore. I fit in. I wasn't that geeky kid with the foreign parents. I was somebody cool, or at least I was under the mistaken impression that I was."

"How young were you when you started drinking?"

"Fifteen."

"Were you drinking all the time?" Juliane asked, wondering how young her dad had started.

"In the beginning, I only drank at parties on the weekends. That's pretty much the pattern I followed through my school years—binge drinking on the weekends. But occasionally I drank during the week, too. I was getting my courage from a bottle."

"So are you saying that you alienated your family

with your drinking?" Juliane took the last pretzel and popped it into her mouth.

"Mostly I alienated my grandfather. He was the one trying to reach out to me. My parents had other things on their minds." Lukas let out a harsh breath. "Near the end of my senior year in high school, my mother died of breast cancer. For most of my high school years, my parents were consumed with her illness, and my drinking was pretty much under their radar."

Juliane felt a burst of sympathy. She hadn't known that Lukas had lost his mother. "So are you saying that because of your mother's illness, they weren't paying much attention to you?"

"Yeah, I guess I'm saying that." Lukas grimaced. "After I went to college, my father moved back to Germany. The Berlin Wall had come down, and Germany had been reunited. He wanted to see the family members he'd left behind. With my mother gone, he felt no reason to continue living here."

"How did you feel about that?"

"I was on my way to college. I had my own life to live." Lukas shook his head. "I was selfish, only thinking of myself. As long as my father paid my college tuition, I was happy."

While Juliane listened to Lukas tell his story, she wondered whether something tragic in her father's life had led to his drinking. She'd never considered such a possibility before. "But you weren't really happy, were you?"

"True. In the beginning I used the drinking to be cool, but when my mother died I used it to blunt the pain. Grandpa began to notice, but I didn't listen to anything he said. The more he tried, the harder I pushed him away. So he pretty much washed his hands of me."

"I noticed there's some tension between you. Is it still because of your drinking?"

Lukas sat up and looked at her. "No, no. He knows I'm sober now. The tension you see is all about him wanting his independence. He thinks I'm encroaching on it by my constant attention. But as you see, he needs it."

"And he's fortunate to have you."

"Thanks. I appreciate your saying so."

"If it's any consolation, the way you take care of him has made me see you in a more positive light."

"That's good to hear." A slow smile brightened Lukas's face. "I didn't mean to go on and on about all this, but I didn't want to get off on the wrong foot in this town. I wanted you to understand."

"But you still haven't told me how your former boss helped you." She couldn't believe she was asking him to continue when only a little while before she'd been desperate to leave. Yet she couldn't help but want to hear the rest of his story.

Lukas's shoulders sagged. "You really want to hear more? Are you a glutton for punishment?"

"I guess I am. I really do want to hear about it." She opened one of the candy bars and took a bite.

"I used my one call to phone Bill Martin. For some reason, I still had his card in my wallet."

"How did he react?"

"He told me he'd help me however he could but under one condition. I had to go into rehab."

"Did you agree?"

"Not right away. I had to sit in a jail cell overnight. When I sobered up, I figured it was my best way out."

"So going to rehab was the answer?"

Shaking his head, Lukas smiled wryly. "Not hardly."

"But I thought you said he helped you." Juliane frowned.

"He did, but the rehab didn't work until I finally realized I had to turn my life over to God."

"So how did that happen?"

"I was in and out of rehab three times but after the first two times, I started drinking again."

"Why?"

"I was relying on myself. And when things didn't go right for one reason or another, the temptation to take a drink was too strong. I had nothing to help me resist, and I couldn't do it on my own."

"But I thought you said your friend—your boss— was a Christian. Didn't he tell you how Jesus can help?"

Lukas nodded. "Yeah, he did, but I never bought into the whole religion thing, at least not the first two times I was in rehab even though the counselors there also tried to teach me about relying on God. That was for weaklings, and I was no weakling."

"How long did all of this take?"

"Three years. Every time I came out Bill helped me get a job, but I always got fired because I started drinking again." Lukas's voice trailed off, and he sat in silence for a moment with his head bowed. Then he looked up. "But Bill didn't give up on me, even after I failed."

Juliane had to strain to hear Lukas's words, and she was almost sure she saw tears welling in his eyes. A lump formed in her throat, and for a few seconds she couldn't speak as his testimony about his friend and Lukas's obvious gratitude touched her. "So what made you finally decide to change?"

"When I saw how Bill believed in me when no one else did, I knew I couldn't let him down again. He stood by me and told me God would, too, if I'd just give Him a chance."

"Did your friend insist that you go back to rehab the second and third times?" Juliane asked.

"No, but every time I failed to do it on my own I went back. I wanted to get better. I really did. I thank God I had someone like Bill to help me."

"So your friend's persistence made a difference?"

"It did. He made a huge difference. He wouldn't give up until I saw my need for God." Lukas paused and finished off the bag of pretzels, then took a deep breath. "Now I don't know how I ever lived without God in my life. I'm not saying I'm never tempted, and I'm not saying it's easy. But now I have a source of strength I never had before."

Juliane was glad for Lukas that someone had helped him, but it made her wonder. Her dad was a Christian and attended church regularly, so why couldn't he rely on God? What kept him from tapping that source of power to overcome the drinking? She was almost tempted to talk to Lukas about it, but he was still more of a stranger than a friend.

Despite Lukas's struggle with alcohol, she couldn't open up to him about her father. Deep down she was ashamed to admit that her father wasn't as strong as Lukas, that he hadn't been able to bring himself to do what Lukas had done. And what about her? If she'd been more like Bill Martin, would she have been able to help her father?

"So you really find a source of strength from God?"

"Don't you?"

"After listening to you—maybe not as much as I should. I guess I see all too often people who are supposed to be Christians not living the way they are supposed to live. Sometimes that includes me." Juliane was learning a lesson from a very unlikely source. The discussion hit her right where she was struggling to let God's power into her life—her embarrassment over her father's alcoholism.

"I don't know what to tell you. I can't speak for other people. I know how it works for me. God is my anchor. I memorized these verses from Psalm 118 when I was in rehab. 'I was pushed back and about to fall, but the Lord helped me. The Lord is my strength and my song; He has become my salvation.'"

"Those are great verses. Guess I should put them to memory, too."

"They mean a lot to me. I'm sure you've heard the one-day-at-a-time thing for people dealing with addictions. Well, it's true. It's like walking a tightrope. You have to put one foot in front of the other over and over again. You can't look down—so to speak. You have to keep your eyes on Jesus. Those verses remind me."

"Thanks." Juliane touched Lukas's arm. "Thanks for sharing this with me."

"I wanted to do it so you'd look at me differently. I don't like to go around broadcasting that I'm an alcoholic. I was hoping by setting things straight with you that all this could stay in the past and not be brought up now."

Juliane instantly knew what he meant. "You might have one more person to deal with besides me."

"Who?"

"My cousin Nathan. He knew you in college, too."

"Would I have seen him since I've moved to town?"

Juliane shrugged. "I don't know. He's vice president at the locally owned bank and goes to church with us. He's in the choir, but he's been busy lately and hasn't had time to attend practice. He and I usually sing the lead parts when the choir has a special program."

"So you're saying I got the part Nathan usually has? I suppose that didn't make you happy." Lukas gave her a questioning look.

"I never said that."

"But you thought it."

"Okay. I did." She grimaced and hoped he wouldn't hold it against her.

She could see now that he truly had changed and felt guilty for her initial suspicions. But still she cautioned herself not to let his confession and explanations make her like him too much. He still wasn't what she was looking for in her life. He was too attractive, too compelling. Men like that went for Elise, not her. Elise…who would be in town soon, and who would have the chance to catch Lukas's eye. And after that, Juliane wouldn't stand a chance. She had no business entertaining romantic thoughts about Lukas Frey. That scenario could lead to trouble—and most likely heartbreak down the road.

"Does Nathan remember me? Should I remember him?"

Juliane shrugged. "I have no idea. I haven't spoken to him since I returned from my buying trip. I thought he would be at choir practice last Wednesday, but he wasn't."

"So I got the part by default?"

"No. You got it because you deserved it. You'll do a good job."

"Thanks for your confidence."

"Just stating fact. Remember, I've heard you sing before."

"All those years ago when I wasn't quite sober?"

"You sing well under any circumstances."

"Maybe." Releasing a harsh breath, Lukas stared at her. "I hate thinking about the wasted years."

Juliane nibbled on the last of her candy bar as she listened to him. She couldn't believe how much her perception of him had changed in one evening. Yet she wasn't quite sure how to respond to her new opinion of him. She wasn't even sure how to respond to his comment. How could she figure this out?

Finishing the last of her cola, she realized she was forgetting the main thing—the thing Lukas had been talking about all night. The Lord was her strength. *Lord, please help me.*

"You've suddenly gotten very quiet. I didn't mean to make you uncomfortable with all my confessions." Lukas shifted in his chair and drained the last of his cola.

Did she dare tell him the problem lay with her, not him? Maybe they should talk about something else. "I'm just thinking."

"About what?"

"About what you've said. I'm glad you wanted me to understand. And you've made me examine some things about myself." Juliane hoped the discussion could end here. "Should we talk about the banquet entertainment? After all, that was the original intent of this evening."

"Sure."

Before Juliane could say another word, one of the emergency-room doctors came through the double doors and approached Lukas. "Mr. Frey, we've finished examining your grandfather. I'd like for you to step into the room while we explain to him what we've found."

Lukas popped up from his chair. "Is he going to be okay?"

"Let's all talk together." The doctor moved toward the doors.

As Lukas followed, he turned to Juliane. "You can come, too."

Juliane shook her head. "No, this should be just you, your grandfather and the doctor. You can fill me in later, if you want."

"Okay." Lukas hurried after the doctor, the double doors closing behind him.

Juliane sank back onto the chair and bowed her

head. *Lord, please be with Ferd and keep him safe. Please be with Lukas and keep him strong. Don't let this crisis derail him from his sobriety. And help me be the friend that he needs.*

The minutes dragged, but finally Lukas returned. His ashen face told her that the news wasn't good. Her heart in her throat, she rushed over to him. "What's happened?"

"The tests confirmed that Grandpa had a heart attack. He has a blocked artery. They're going to transfer him to Cincinnati where they can do an angioplasty. They aren't equipped to do one here."

"How soon?"

"Right away. As soon as the helicopter arrives." Lukas fished his car keys from one of his pockets. "I'm going to drive ahead to the hospital in Cincinnati. I'll meet them there."

"Is there anything I can do?" For an instant Juliane wanted to give Lukas a hug, but she pushed the urge away. She didn't need to go there.

"Just pray."

"You know I will."

"Do you want me to call a taxi for you?"

"No need to worry about me." Juliane pulled her BlackBerry from her purse. "I'll give my mom a call right now. She'll come and take me to my car."

"That's fine. I'd better get going." Lukas raced out the door.

BlackBerry in hand, Juliane ran after him. "Call me anytime to let me know how things are going."

"Sure." He waved as he got into his car.

Forgetting about the cold, Juliane watched him drive away. She'd learned a lot about Lukas tonight. Everything he'd told her made him more likable. He'd been sober for six years—way longer than her father had ever been. She could so easily start to like him too much for her own good, but she would reserve judgment. He would have to earn her trust. Her experience with her father told her that too often alcoholics told you what they thought you wanted to hear. They made all kinds of promises but never delivered.

Chapter Five

The steady beep, beep, beep of the heart monitor had an almost hypnotic quality as Lukas stared at the numbers and lines on the display screen. Nearly forty-eight hours had passed since he'd taken his grandfather to the emergency room. The angioplasty had gone well, and his grandfather rested peacefully in the nearby hospital bed.

Lukas had bought a book in the hospital gift shop, but he couldn't concentrate long enough to read more than a few pages at a time. His eyes were constantly drawn to the monitor and the jagged lines that indicated his grandfather's heartbeat.

A knock sounded on the door, taking Lukas's attention away from the monitor. He glanced up.

Looking great in a pair of gray slacks, a cable-knit sweater and a warm smile, Juliane stood in the doorway. "May I come in?"

"Sure." Jumping up from his chair, Lukas waved his hand for her to join him. "This is a surprise."

"I hope it's okay for Ferd to have visitors."

"It is, but right now he's sleeping."

"Should we come back later?"

"We?"

"Yeah, my folks are with me." Juliane motioned toward the hall. "I was just checking before we all barged in."

"Your folks know my grandfather?" Lukas wondered whether Juliane had given her parents the lowdown on his past. Was that question going to plague him every time he met one of Juliane's acquaintances?

"My mom does. We're going to dinner here in Cincinnati. So we thought we'd stop by and see how Ferd's doing."

Looking at Juliane, Lukas realized how glad he was to see her—something that wasn't going to help him keep his interest in her in check. "How does your mom know him?"

"Since Ferd's sleeping, why don't you come out to the waiting room with me? I'll introduce you to my mother, then she can tell you how she knows him. We can visit with my parents until he wakes up."

Lukas glanced back at his grandfather. He hadn't moved. The heart monitor still indicated a good steady heartbeat. Turning back to Juliane, Lukas wondered whether he was up for this meeting. He'd already met her father, but that was before he understood his relation to Juliane.

Why was he suddenly tying himself in knots about meeting new people? Dumb question. He knew the answer. He wanted to make a good impression. Because they might know about his past? Yes…but also because he wanted to give Juliane another reason to smile at him, warmly and sincerely, the way she had just moments ago. Why was he always thinking about himself? These people were here to see his grandfather, not him. "I suppose I can leave him for a few minutes."

Juliane led the way into the hall. "Have you been here the whole time?"

"No, I've stepped out to eat but stayed nearby the room most of the time. I did go to a hotel last night, but my sleep was pretty restless."

"Are you okay?"

Rubbing the stubble on his chin, Lukas realized what he must look like—unshaven and disheveled. Although he'd showered this morning, he hadn't bothered to shave because he'd never counted on visitors. "Yeah, but I know I look terrible."

"Not terrible, but tired. How much sleep did you get?"

"Not much. I kept waking up and worrying about Grandpa." Lukas didn't relish this encounter. What kind of an impression was he going to make? He should be beyond caring at this point, but for some reason he wasn't. He wanted Juliane's parents to like him.

"I can understand. I don't think I would've gotten much sleep either."

As Lukas trailed Juliane down the hallway, he spotted her father sitting next to a middle-aged woman with short light brown hair that was liberally sprinkled with gray. They stood as Juliane drew near. He braced for the meeting and reminded himself that they were here because of his grandfather, so he should get over himself.

Lukas shook Ray Keller's hand. Then Ray introduced his wife, Barbara. Ray and his wife were a picture of contrast. Not one gray hair marked Ray's brown hair, and where he was a little thick around the middle and very tall, his wife was petite and trim. Although Juliane was taller than her mother, Lukas saw the resemblance between them immediately.

Barbara shook Lukas's hand, then placed her other hand over his and squeezed it. "I'm pleased to meet you. We're so sorry to hear about your grandfather, but we're glad you got him to the hospital before things got worse."

"Me, too." Lukas glanced at Juliane. "And I appreciate Juliane's help."

Juliane gave him a little smile. "It was nothing."

"Good thing Juliane called me so we could start the prayer chain." Barbara released Lukas's hand. "I met your grandfather when our ladies' circle from church helped with a holiday party at the senior center last month. How is he doing?"

"As well as can be expected. The angioplasty went according to plan, and he's sleeping now."

"I hope we get to see him before we have to leave. We stopped by on our way to dinner," Barbara said.

"Yes, Juliane told me."

Barbara smiled. "Juliane tells me you have the male lead in the Winter Festival program. She says you have a wonderful singing voice."

Lukas wondered whether that was all Juliane had said about him. He looked her way. "Thank you."

Juliane glanced at her mother, then back at Lukas. "Mom didn't realize at first who I was talking about when I told her about Ferd, but she finally made the connection when I mentioned the senior center."

"Grandpa certainly loves going there. I'm glad there's a place like that for him. Otherwise, I think he'd sit in the house all day and watch TV."

"Does he attend church anywhere?" Barbara asked.

"He used to, but his hearing got so bad that he quit going. He said he couldn't hear anyway, so he started listening to preachers on TV." Lowering his head, Lukas rubbed the back of his neck. "I had intended to set up an appointment for him to see about getting hearing aids before all this happened."

"Can the senior center help him find a place to get

a hearing aid?" Barbara looked at Juliane. "I think they have information about that kind of thing, don't they?"

"Yes, I think they do." Juliane glanced from her mother to Lukas. "I'll look into it for you."

"Thanks." Lukas couldn't get over Juliane's helpfulness. Another reason not to think of her romantically. She was becoming too important to him as a friend. He wondered what she thought after he'd run off at the mouth the other night. Afterward he couldn't believe he'd practically told her his life's story—almost every disgusting detail. Maybe it was the stress of his grandfather's emergency that had him talking to her so openly. But she'd been so easy to talk to—so easy to like.

"Did he attend where we go?" Juliane's question brought him back to the present. "I don't recall seeing him there."

"No. He went to another church."

"When he's better, you should bring him with you. We have special earphones for the hearing impaired." Juliane glanced at her mom. "They even have someone who teaches sign language, if he's interested in learning. The ladies' circle started that ministry a couple of years ago, didn't they, Mom?"

"Yes, they did. We have several seniors who use the earphones. They say it really helps them." Barbara glanced at the chairs behind them. "Should we sit down?"

"Good idea." Ray settled on one of the chairs covered in a brown tweed material. "Lukas, how are things going at the plant?"

"Everything's right on schedule, but I'm taking off work until I can get my grandfather settled into the nursing home back in Kellersburg." Sighing, Lukas shook his head. "He doesn't understand why he can't go home."

Barbara nodded. "It's always hard when an older person has to go to a nursing home. How long will he have to stay?"

"Probably not more than a week. I want to make sure he can take care of himself." Lukas glanced down the hall and wondered whether he should go check on his grandfather again. After all, Grandpa was the one they'd really come to see. "I'd like him to live with me, but he wants to be on his own. He won't consider it."

"It's hard for older folks to give up their independence. Ray and I have both dealt with that kind of thing with our parents." Barbara patted Juliane's arm. "Juliane here has been such a help to us. She ran the store while we were taking care of Ray's parents. We're so glad she decided to return to Kellersburg after she graduated from college."

Lukas took in the praise Barbara heaped on her daughter. He envied Juliane's relationship with her parents. He barely had contact with his father these days. So taking care of his grandfather was on the top of his list. He hoped he was doing the right things to preserve that relationship.

Lukas also wondered about Juliane's sister and how she fit into their family, since she'd been away for so long. The more he learned about Juliane the more she intrigued him. But he couldn't act on his interest. He had other things—a job and his grandfather—to take care of now. Besides, even if she could forgive him for his past, she'd never want to be with someone like him.

Lukas stood. "I'm going to check on my grandfather. Do you want to wait here?"

"I think that would be best," Barbara replied.

"If he's awake, I'll come back and get you." Lukas pulled his BlackBerry from his pocket and glanced at it. "How long before you have to leave for your dinner engagement?"

Ray looked at his watch. "We have about an hour."

"Good." Lukas started down the hall. "I'll be back in a minute."

Lukas wondered what Juliane and her parents would talk about while he was gone. Would they talk about him? *Quit thinking about yourself.* Stopping for a moment, he took a deep breath. He was tying himself in knots for no good reason. *Lord, help me to put this all in Your hands. I'm not doing so well on my own.*

As Lukas arrived at his grandfather's room, a

nurse was leaving. She smiled. "I just checked on your grandfather. He's doing great. In a little while, we'll get him up for a walk."

"So he's awake?"

"He is." The nurse bustled away, chart in hand.

Lukas stuck his head around the door frame. "Hi, Grandpa. You have visitors. Do you feel like entertaining company?"

The older man nodded. "I could use some new scenery. All I see is you and those nurses."

Chuckling, Lukas hurried back down the hallway toward the waiting area. Juliane smiled as he approached, and his heart seemed to jump around like the lines on his grandfather's heart monitor. Trying to tamp down the reaction, he took a calming breath. She shouldn't make him feel this way. Who was he trying to kid? She'd had his attention from the moment he'd seen her at choir practice. She had his emotions jumping through hoops.

He forced himself to look at her father, who stood as Lukas motioned for them to come. "He's awake and ready for visitors."

"I'm so glad we get to see him before we have to go." Juliane hurried up beside Lukas and plucked a package from her purse. "I brought him a little gift."

"You're going to spoil him."

"He deserves spoiling."

"I don't know about that. He's already hard to deal with without you spoiling him." Lukas laughed.

When Juliane and her parents entered the room, his grandfather smiled. Juliane went over to the bed and took one of his gnarled hands in hers. "You are looking wonderful."

"You are so sweet to an old man." Ferd beamed.

Lukas took in the way Juliane grasped his grandfather's hand and wished he were in his grandfather's place. Lukas shook the image away. He had to quit thinking about Juliane in the context of romance. How many times had he thought that since Juliane and her parents had arrived? Too many.

Then he remembered the other night and how his grandfather had made the pronouncement about Juliane making Lukas a good wife. Oh, great. He hoped his grandfather wouldn't start his matchmaking again, especially in front of her parents.

Juliane quickly introduced her father to Ferd, then produced the little package she'd shown Lukas. "Here's a little something to occupy your time."

"Thank you. You didn't have to bring me a gift."

"I know, but I wanted to." Juliane's eyes lit up with pleasure. She clearly enjoyed giving. "Go ahead. Open it."

Ferd tore into the paper, revealing a crossword puzzle book. "How did you know I liked to do crossword puzzles?"

"I saw one sitting on the table next to the recliner in your living room the other night."

"You are a brilliant young woman." Ferd winked at her.

Lukas had to admit he was losing the battle to keep himself neutral when it came to Juliane Keller. He let that thought roll around in his brain while he listened to Juliane, her parents and his grandfather engaged in a lively conversation. He said a prayer of thanks that folks like the Kellers cared enough to come and visit. He thanked God for another day of sobriety that let him be there for his grandfather and enjoy the company of friends.

Eventually Lukas joined the conversation. Despite the worry over his attraction to Juliane, he liked the Kellers and hoped they would find more occasions to visit. They were already helping him feel a bond with their community. In such a short time, Kellersburg was feeling like home.

"Well, it's time for us to get going. We have to meet these people for dinner." Ray extended his hand to Ferd. "You take care of yourself and get better soon."

Ferd shook Ray's hand. "I will. That grandson of mine won't give me any other choice. He's got his nose in everything I do."

Chuckling, Barbara gave Ferd's arm a pat. "He's taken good care of you. So listen to him."

"He has to. He can't get rid of me." Lukas shook hands with Ray. "Thanks so much for stopping by."

"Let us know when you're back in Kellersburg." Juliane leaned over and gave Ferd a kiss on the forehead. "Be good."

"All this advice and a kiss from a pretty girl, too." Ferd beamed.

Lukas tried not to think of kissing Juliane himself. He had to wipe that thought out of his brain before it had time to settle. He was headed for dangerous territory—territory he hadn't explored in a long, long time. He was pretty sure he wasn't ready for any such adventure. But as he watched them leave, one question dominated his thoughts. When would he see Juliane again?

The scent of pine cleaner did nothing to cover the medicinal smell associated with illness as Juliane entered the nursing home. Walking the hallway lined with residents in wheelchairs—some lucid, some not—she couldn't help thinking about Ferd's distaste for being here. He had made that quite clear when she'd visited him after work the past two days. She could imagine that Ferd gave Lukas an earful every time he came to visit.

Today, she'd taken off work a little early so she could fit her visit in before she went to choir practice. She'd been gearing herself up all day for the upcoming encounter with Lukas. She'd prayed about it, but sometimes she felt as though her prayers never reached beyond her mind. Why was God feeling so far away these days?

Both Monday and Tuesday evenings she'd met Lukas as she was leaving and he was coming to the nursing home. And even though she'd spent hours having a lengthy conversation with him while they were at the hospital, somehow the impending inter-action was on a whole different level—one for which she wasn't prepared.

The thought of another extended encounter with him had her trying to decipher her mixed-up feelings. She'd managed to spend a couple of minutes making small talk with him the past two nights before they'd gone their separate ways, but she wasn't sure how she would cope with the two-hour choir practice.

The thought of singing with him had her emotions as jumbled as the letters in the new word search book she'd bought for Ferd. The kindness that Lukas showed to his grandfather drew her in, but she was still uncertain about him. What did he want from her? Forgiveness? Friendship? More? What was she willing to offer? Could she ever reconcile these con-flicting thoughts?

Deciding would be much easier if he wasn't so heart-stopping gorgeous.

Deep in thought, she plowed into Ferd's room,

then did a double take when she realized Lukas sat in the chair next to his grandfather's bed. Ferd occupied the other chair in his half of the semiprivate room. Her heart nearly stopped and then started racing as she stared at Lucas's handsome, smiling face.

He stood. "Hi, there."

What are you doing here? The words almost tumbled out of her mouth, but she managed to regain her senses before she spoke. "Hi. I'm surprised to see you here."

"I left work a little early because I wanted to make sure I had time to visit Grandpa before choir practice." Lukas motioned to the chair where he'd been sitting. "You can have my seat. I'll sit here on the bed."

"Thanks." Juliane went over and gave Ferd a hug. "You are looking better every day."

"Not because of the food they're serving." Ferd waved a hand toward his half-eaten meal. "Gelatin again. I wonder what flavor I'll get tomorrow."

Juliane chuckled. "It can't be that bad."

"Well, maybe not, but I'm ready to get out of here." Ferd nodded toward Lukas. "Tell that grandson of mine."

Juliane glanced at Lukas. He appeared unmoved by his grandfather's plea. "I don't think Lukas has much say in the matter, do you?"

Lukas grinned. "Not really. I'm taking my cue from the therapists and the docs."

His grin made her legs feel like the gelatin on Ferd's dinner tray. She immediately sat in the nearby chair to get off her wobbly legs. This was crazy. Why was she reacting this way now? She'd been so determined not to fall for him. There was only one conclusion. She'd spent far too much time thinking about Lukas today.

"I brought you another book. This one's a word search." Juliane handed it to Ferd.

"You are too good to me—unlike my grandson."

Juliane patted Ferd's hand. "Lukas has been very good to you. You should appreciate him."

"I'll appreciate him when he springs me from this place."

"Thanks." Lukas smiled at her.

"You're welcome," Juliane said with a sense of satisfaction warming her. Maybe this wasn't going to be so bad after all. "Has the doctor indicated when Ferd can go home?"

Ferd was about to open his mouth, but Lukas glared his grandfather into silence. "Maybe Friday."

"That's sooner than you expected, right?"

"Yes, but still not soon enough for me." Ferd tapped himself on the chest.

"Grandpa, just be satisfied it'll probably be Friday." Lukas sighed. "I've scheduled an appointment for you to see about hearing aids, too."

"Another annoyance." Ferd frowned.

Rolling his eyes, Lukas stood. "Let's take a walk and get a little exercise."

"That sounds like an excellent idea. I could use the exercise myself." Juliane hopped up from her chair and hoped Ferd wouldn't give Lukas any more grief. Maybe it was the grandson-grandfather relationship that caused Ferd to be so uncooperative. He was never grouchy and uncooperative at the senior center. Or maybe his attitude was the result of his health problems.

Ferd pushed himself up from his chair. "If it means getting out of this place sooner, I'm all for it."

Ferd led the way while Juliane and Lukas strolled behind him through the halls of the nursing home. Ferd used his cane, but he was moving right along without any trouble. Lukas hung back with Juliane as Ferd continued to forge ahead, stopping occasionally to visit with one of the other residents or one of the nurses. He laughed and talked, and Juliane saw the man she knew from the senior center emerge from behind the cantankerous facade he displayed whenever he was conversing with Lukas.

"Now that's the Ferd I know," Juliane whispered to Lukas as they observed at a distance.

"Yeah, I seem to bring out the worst in him." Lukas laughed halfheartedly. "At least lately."

"I'm sure things will get better once he leaves here."

"I hope so."

While Juliane walked beside Lukas through the

nursing home, she realized her discomfort with being around him had subsided. She wasn't completely comfortable, but her attitude was a whole lot better. She was on his side as he dealt with his grandfather. God was answering her prayers in His own time. He was making her see that she'd been praying but trying to take care of her problems on her own rather than relying on Him to take care of them.

After they'd traversed every hallway in the nursing home, they returned to Ferd's room. Just as he settled on his chair, two white-haired women appeared at the door. Juliane recognized them from the senior center.

Ferd immediately stood again, a wide smile on his face. "Dot, Evelyn, it is so nice of you to visit me. I'm glad to see you."

"We were just stopping by to say hello, but we see you already have company." Dot, the shorter of the two women, started to retreat.

Lukas stepped aside and motioned for them to come in. "That's okay. There's plenty of room in here. Besides, Juliane and I have been here a while, and we have to get to choir practice. So this is a good time for us to leave and let you visit with one another."

The two women proceeded into the room, and Juliane introduced them to Lukas. Then Juliane and Lukas bade goodbye to Ferd and stepped into the hallway.

As Juliane bustled toward the exit, Lukas fell into step beside her. "Are you always in such a hurry?"

She glanced over at him. "I just walk fast."

"You managed to keep a slower pace when we walked with Grandpa tonight."

"Well, that was different." Juliane narrowed her gaze as she felt a little of her old irritation return. She quickly tamped it down. Lukas didn't need her prickliness on top of Ferd's.

He grinned at her. "I was only kidding."

"I'm sorry—"

"You're forgiven," he interrupted. "I'm starved. How about getting something to eat?"

Chapter Six

Juliane's first reaction was to decline, but his invitation was another test of her resolve to deal with Lukas and all of her conflicting emotions about him. "Okay, but it has to be somewhere fast."

"Fast food?"

"No, just fast service."

"Is there someplace in town where we can get a quick meal without going to a fast-food restaurant?" he asked.

"Yeah, follow me." Juliane headed for her car.

Minutes later, Lukas joined her as they approached a café on Main Street, not far from the church. "One of my dad's cousins runs this place."

They slid into the booth with dark faux-leather seats, and the waitress immediately appeared and handed them menus. Lukas looked his over, then glanced up. "What do you recommend?"

"I always get the chicken fingers basket."

"Okay. I'll go with your recommendation." He closed his menu as the waitress returned to take their order.

"I hope I didn't steer you wrong," Juliane said after the waitress left.

"I'm sure you didn't, but in case you did, you have an in with the management." Lukas chuckled. "Does your family own everything in town?"

"No, only half of it." Juliane laughed, then shook her head. "I'm only kidding. My family owns a lot of the older businesses in town because they've been passed down through the generations, but things have changed in the past ten years."

"How so?"

"More people moving in from the city. We've really become a bedroom community for Cincinnati." Juliane took the napkin off the flatware. "New businesses have sprung up all over town. The plant you run is new."

"So how do the folks around here feel about all the changes?"

"Some think they're good. Some think they're bad. That's the way it is with any change." Juliane thought of the change Lukas's presence had brought to her own thinking. "You have to adjust."

"And how have you adjusted?"

"You mean me personally?" What was he getting

at? Did he realize how she was struggling since he'd arrived in town?

"You personally and your store."

"We had to make a number of changes when the big discount store opened on the outskirts of town." Juliane picked up her fork as the waitress brought their order.

"That was quick."

"I told you the service is fast."

"Would you like me to give thanks?"

"Sure." Bowing her head, Juliane put down her fork, embarrassed that she hadn't considered praying.

For a few minutes after the prayer, they ate in silence. Juliane's mind wrapped around one thing for sure. Being with Lukas was getting her more in touch with God. In her wildest imagination, she never would have believed Lukas could be the one to help with her spiritual life.

Lukas took a big gulp of his drink, then eyed her. "Tell me about the changes you've made in order to compete with the discount store."

Juliane reflected for a moment. Leave it to Lukas to ask something that brought into focus all the problems she had with her father. "Most of the changes had to do with the kind of merchandise stocked. I had a terrible time trying to convince my dad that we couldn't compete with the discount store with the lines we were carrying."

"Is your dad as stubborn as my grandfather?"

Juliane nodded. "Actually, a lot of times I made the changes without consulting him. When the changes did well, he didn't complain."

"I can see you doing that." Lukas laughed.

"And what is that supposed to mean?"

"You are determined, and when you want something, nothing is going to stand in your way. I can tell that by the way you walk."

"You judge people by the way they walk?"

"Sometimes. Body language can tell you a lot about people."

"Speaking of body language, did you notice the way your grandfather's eyes lit up when he looked at Dot tonight?"

"No. Are you sure?"

"Absolutely. You mean Mr. Body Language Expert missed a clue?"

Lukas shrugged. "I guess, if you're right. I don't see Grandpa having a romantic interest in any woman. He's been a widower for nearly forty years, and as far as I know, he's never even taken a woman out on a date."

"Maybe he just never met the right woman before."

"No." Lukas vehemently shook his head as he finished off his chicken fingers. "He told everyone time and time again that no one could replace his Anna. My grandmother died before I was born, before the escape from East Germany. Breast cancer—just like my mother. Good thing I didn't have a sister."

Sorrow and pain radiated from Lukas's words. She couldn't imagine what it would be like to lose her mother even now, much less as a teenager. For an instant Juliane was tempted to reach across the table and cover his hand with hers. But she held her hands tightly in her lap. She couldn't let herself be drawn into his life any more than she already had. "I'm so sorry about your grandmother and your mother."

"Thanks. I didn't mean to be such a downer." Lukas pulled his BlackBerry out of his coat pocket. "We'd better get the check and be on our way to practice."

"Don't worry about it. I'm glad you told me." Juliane picked up her purse and slid out of the booth. "Our check's already been taken care of."

Standing beside Juliane, Lukas knit his eyebrows in a little frown. "How's that?"

"Remember, my dad's cousin owns the place."

"Are you saying the meal was on him?"

"No, I just said the bill's been taken care of."

"You are a sneaky one." Lukas grinned. "I'll take care of the bill next time."

Heading for the door, Juliane wondered what that meant. Did he plan on taking her out to dinner another time? Why did the prospect worry her and excite her at the same time? This was not good.

Lukas opened the door and waited for Juliane to

go outside. "Do you really think there's something going on with my grandfather and Dot?"

"Your guess is as good as mine. We'll have to wait and see." Juliane hurried down the sidewalk to her car, which was parked next to Lukas's. She slowed down when she remembered his comment about her speedy pace. "I'll see you in a few minutes."

"Don't drive as fast as you walk." Grinning, he hopped into his car and closed the door.

Sitting in her car for a moment, Juliane couldn't forget the way Lukas had looked when he'd told her about his mother and grandmother. The tiny soft spot that had found its way into her heart over the previous days grew a little. She was beginning to understand him so much more. He'd been through a lot, and he was now relying on God—something she'd neglected to do lately.

Everything about her interaction with Lukas today had been positive—preparing her for choir practice tonight. Had she finally turned the corner with him, or would her old feelings of discomfort return without warning? If she was making progress on this front maybe she was ready for the next big challenge—dealing with Elise's return.

Airline passengers streamed up the escalators as Juliane and her parents searched the crowd for Elise. Juliane's mind buzzed with anticipation. A gamut of emotions washed over her. Anxiety reigned above the rest of them. Juliane tried to push the negative attitude away, but it returned with a vengeance every time she thought about her sister's homecoming. There had always been an unhealthy competition between them. How would they get along after all this time?

Juliane had agreed to share her house with Elise. Now Juliane wondered about the wisdom of that decision. Everything about her life seemed out of control lately. She hated that feeling. She lived for stability, but the events of the past few weeks had tested her ability to lead an orderly life. She couldn't put her interactions with Lukas and Elise into neat little boxes.

Nothing was working out the way she'd planned. She enjoyed living alone, but she felt obligated to share her house with Elise. Now the peace and quiet of her day-to-day life was at risk.

Then there was Lukas. Although everything at choir practice was going smoothly, Juliane was tying herself in knots over her feelings for him. Nothing was tidy about trying to figure out what they meant— why one minute she liked him and the next she worried about getting too close.

Elise was coming home for good, and Lukas was constantly in her thoughts. Juliane wondered how she was supposed to cope when her life was turning upside down. Wasn't that why she was supposed to be trusting in God?

"There she is." Juliane's mom rushed forward, waving her hand above her head.

Juliane hung back as her parents hurried to embrace her sister. Elise, her long curly brown hair accented with honey strands, dropped her backpack and fell into their arms. Juliane felt left out, but the feeling was of her own making. No one was keeping her at a distance. She was doing it to herself.

When her parents stepped back, Elise's brandy-colored eyes found Juliane. The haggard look on Elise's face surprised Juliane as she stepped forward to hug her sister.

Elise held Juliane tight. The embrace lasted longer than Juliane had anticipated, almost as if Elise didn't want to let go. Holding her sister, Juliane realized how thin Elise was. Haggard. Pale. Was Elise ill? Was that why she hadn't signed another contract with the cruise line?

Elise let go of Juliane and stepped back. "It's so good to be home." Elise laughed and hugged Juliane again. "You don't know how good."

"We're glad you're back." Despite her misgivings about her sister's return, Juliane realized she really meant it. But she was concerned about Elise and wanted to ask her why she looked so tired. Maybe the long day's travel had exhausted her? "Are you worn-out from the trip?"

"I am. I'll probably fall asleep in the car on the way

home. Maybe I'll fall asleep just waiting for my baggage." Elise laughed again and gave Juliane another quick hug.

At least it appeared that Elise was in good spirits, despite her long trip. They walked leisurely to the baggage claim as their parents peppered Elise with questions about her trip. When they reached the right area, they stood in silence for a few moments as they searched for the correct carousel.

"This is it." Ray stepped closer to the empty carousel, then turned to Elise. "What are your intentions now that you're home? Do you plan to get a job?"

"I'm planning to move in with Juliane. I thought you knew that. Didn't she tell you?" Elise looked at Juliane with concern.

Ray nodded. "She did, but I wondered about your plans for the future, not just your living arrangements."

"I'm going back to school and finishing my music education degree."

Barbara clasped her hands together as a big smile curved her mouth. "What wonderful news. When will you start?"

"As soon as classes resume for the semester." Elise wrinkled her brow. "I can't remember the exact date, but it's next week."

"So soon? When did you have time to register?" Ray asked.

"I did it all online as soon as I decided not to sign another contract with the cruise line."

"Why didn't you tell us your plans?" Ray eyed his younger daughter.

Elise eyed him back. "I wanted to do this on my own—no interference from well-meaning people like you." Laughing, she poked her dad in the ribs.

"Okay, I get the message—no interference from the old man. Are they going to accept all your old credits?" Chuckling, he shook his head.

Elise gave him a cheesy grin. "Yes, I checked on that, too. So I'm all set."

"What do you intend to live on?" Ray asked.

"My good looks." Elise did a little pirouette with her arms held wide. When she came to a stop, she grinned at her dad.

"I'm serious, girl."

Juliane took in her father's questioning with surprise. She was used to being grilled by her father, but hardly remembered him ever grilling Elise. Maybe she had a selective memory.

"Me, too, Dad." Elise slipped her arm through her dad's and smiled up at him. At nearly six foot, she was only inches shorter than he was. "I hope you're in need of some part-time help at the store."

"That's Juliane's department." He patted Juliane's back.

Juliane grimaced. "You know we always cut

back on help after the holiday season, but I'll see what I can do."

"Thanks, Jules." Elise gave Juliane another hug.

As Elise continued to tease their dad, Juliane's reservations about her sister's return came into sharp focus. Elise had a habit of waltzing into a situation and expecting everything to go smoothly for her. And somehow it always did—or at least, that's the way it had always seemed to Juliane. This job thing was just another example of it. Everything always worked out for Elise, and she never seemed to realize that the world didn't work that way for everyone else.

Elise could always sweet-talk their dad, but she'd never made any effort to stop him when it came to his drinking. She acted as though the problem didn't matter. So Juliane and her mother were left to deal with the consequences and cover for him. They'd been taking care of this while Elise spent six years gallivanting around the world.

As the carousel started moving and luggage began to appear, Juliane took a deep breath. She was falling into the old traps. She didn't want that to happen, but how could she ignore the way Elise behaved? This was not a Christian attitude, and she should pray about it. But right now she wasn't in much of a praying mood.

Juliane told herself these feelings were only temporary. She'd get over them in time…or would she? She pushed the troubling thoughts into a dark corner of her mind as she helped retrieve Elise's bags.

Lifting a large black bag, Juliane groaned. "What do you have in here?"

Shrugging, Elise laughed. "Who knows? I don't remember what I packed in any of the suitcases. I was cramming stuff here and there just to get it all in."

"How many more pieces of luggage do you have?" Ray surveyed the bags surrounding him.

Elise pointed, silently counting the bags. "Two more."

"That's good. Otherwise, I'm not sure we'd have enough room to take them all home." Barbara looked pointedly at Elise. "It's a good thing we're all here to help you get this luggage to the car."

Elise went over and put an arm around her diminutive mother. "It's so good to have us all together."

"That's the truth." Ray's voice boomed above the cacophony of sounds echoing through the baggage claim area. "We should celebrate. I think we should have a big party to welcome Elise home." He turned to his wife. "What do you think, honey?"

Barbara clapped her hands. "That is a marvelous idea. All your cousins, aunts and uncles and old friends would love to celebrate. Maybe we can rent the church hall."

"Mom, Dad, you don't have to make a big fuss."

Elise grabbed the remaining bag off the carousel. "I don't want you going to a lot of trouble."

"No trouble. It'll be fun." Barbara rubbed her hands together. "Are we ready to go?"

Elise nodded. "Looks like we have it all."

"Everyone grab two bags, and I'll take this duffel, as well." Ray slung the strap over his shoulder and led the way to the car, pulling the wheeled bags behind him.

Trailing the others, Juliane fought against the jealousy that seeped into her heart as she listened to her parents plan a party for Elise. They'd never planned a party for her. Hadn't she been the dutiful daughter, taking care of the store, being there whenever her parents had needed her? At least she had to give Elise credit for not pushing the party, although it was a given now that their dad had come up with the idea. Juliane vowed not to let her bad attitude ruin this reunion for her parents.

"I can't believe how much I've missed this place." Elise flung herself onto Juliane's couch as their parents left.

"My house?" Juliane took in the pile of luggage littering her living room and wished Elise would at least take it to her bedroom. Their dad had offered to carry it up, but Elise had insisted that she would do it later. Memories of Elise's room when they were in high school made Juliane shudder. She had forgotten what a slob Elise could be. What had she been thinking when she'd agreed to share her house with her sister?

"No, silly, Kellersburg."

"I can't believe you said that." Juliane playfully looked behind the cushions decorating the couch. "What did you do with my sister?"

Elise picked up a cushion and threw it at Juliane. Juliane threw it back. Soon they were tossing cushions and dodging luggage as they fought a mock battle.

Finally, exhausted and laughing, Juliane held her hands in the air. "I give. You win."

"You give up too easy."

Juliane knew that was true where her sister was concerned. Juliane had always let Elise win. Life was simpler that way. "Would you like some help getting your bags into your room?"

Elise waved a hand at Juliane. "Oh, let's wait until tomorrow. Let's relax and enjoy ourselves tonight."

Juliane tamped down the irritation that accompanied Elise's procrastination. "I won't be able to help you tomorrow. I have to be at the store early."

"That's okay. I've got all day tomorrow to work on it. I can do it by myself." Elise resumed her seat on the couch. "So how's Dad been lately? I can't very well ask when we're all talking on the phone together, and I never know who's reading your e-mails."

Juliane wondered whether she would come home from work tomorrow and find all this stuff still sitting here. She determined not to think about it. "If you'd paid attention, you'd know that you could send e-mails to my private account without any worry."

"I know you said that, but I could never remember which one was which." Elise wrinkled her nose.

"Dad's been fine, since last summer. No drinking at all, even through the holidays."

"That's good to hear."

"Everything's been going very well."

Even as she said it, Juliane couldn't help thinking about Lukas. Everything had been going well until he'd shown up and upset the peacefulness of her life. But the changes he'd triggered had been good ones. He'd made her reexamine her reliance on God and her judgmental attitudes. She was seeing them even now in the way she was thinking about Elise. Maybe Elise's return would yield positive results, as well.

"You certainly have gotten your second wind."

"Well, that nap on the way home helped."

"Are you feeling okay?"

"Yeah, why?"

"You've lost a lot of weight, haven't you?" Juliane held her breath while she waited for an answer.

"You noticed?"

"It's very evident." Juliane joined Elise on the couch, forgetting her earlier irritation. "I'm surprised

Mom didn't say something about it. Are you having some health issues? Is that why you quit your job?"

"Wow! Juliane, you're worse than Mom and Dad with the inquisition."

Juliane refused to let her sister redirect the conversation. "Just call me concerned and nosy, and answer the question."

"I'm fine."

"That's hard to believe. How can anyone lose weight on a cruise ship?"

"Easy. You work a lot of hours and don't eat much." Elise stretched out her long legs, encased in a pair of khaki pants.

"Do you have any clothes for cold weather in all those suitcases?" Juliane noticed her sister's light-weight shirt as well as her pants that definitely weren't warm enough for January in Ohio.

"Maybe a couple of things, but I'm sure I can pick some stuff up at the store." Elise glanced around the room. "Hey, do you know you've got a message on your answering machine?"

Turning, Juliane looked into the kitchen where the bright red message light blinked on and off. "I guess I do. How did I not notice before?"

"Too busy talking and getting Mom and Dad out of our hair so we can have some sister time."

Juliane walked into the kitchen and punched the button to play the message.

"Hey, Juliane. It's Lukas. I tried to leave you a message on your mobile, but you never called back. Hope all went well when you picked up your sister. I meant to ask you earlier today about getting together for the entertainment thing, but I forgot. Grandpa's doing great. Give me a call when you can."

As the message ended, Juliane wished she'd discovered the message while she was alone. Now Elise would ask questions in her so-called sister time.

Before Juliane could turn around, Elise was by her side. "So who's Lukas?"

"Just a guy who's helping me with the talent program for the Valentine's banquet."

"Just a guy, huh?"

"Yeah, he's new in town, and Val sort of pushed him into helping me."

"She's matchmaking?"

"You're jumping to a lot of conclusions, aren't you? He could be some old married man."

"But he's not, is he?" Elise grinned.

Juliane sighed. "No, but there's no matchmaking going on. Val was helping him get acquainted with the community."

"Okay, if you say so, but what's this about him seeing you earlier today? And why is he giving you a report on his grandpa?"

"It's a long story."

"I've got plenty of time."

"Okay. I saw him at church this morning."

"Oh, yeah, church. When you travel, you kind of lose track of the days."

"And going to church?"

Elise grimaced. "I'm kind of out of the habit."

"Will that change now that you're home?"

"I suppose it'll have to if you have anything to say about it."

Juliane couldn't miss Elise's little dig, but she wasn't going to let it get to her. "What you do about going to church is between you and God, not me."

"What about his grandfather?" Elise asked, seemingly ignoring Juliane's comment about church.

Juliane proceeded to tell Elise about Lukas and what had happened to his grandfather. "So now are you satisfied that nothing's going on with Lukas and me?"

"Hardly. I can't wait to meet him!"

Out of nowhere, a stab of jealousy hit Juliane. What did she care if Elise met Lukas? She had no claims on him. She didn't even want any. So why was she having these feelings? She had to get over them, and with God's help she would.

Chapter Seven

The next day gray skies foreshadowed the snow that was rolling in from the west. Juliane locked up the store and waved goodbye to her dad, who was on his way to the bank to make a night deposit. She hated gloomy winter days, and this particular gloom only added to her apprehension about sharing her house with Elise.

Juliane had vowed to get over second thoughts. But when she'd stumbled over Elise's luggage on her way to the kitchen this morning, her vow had faded as quickly as the daylight was fading now on this late afternoon.

Light shone through the large picture window in the living room as she pulled into the driveway at the side of her century-old brick house. She punched the button on the garage-door opener. While the door slowly rose, Juliane prepared herself to find Elise still surrounded by a mess of luggage while she watched TV. She had complained of jet lag last night, so Juliane wouldn't be surprised to find her sister still in bed.

I will not be angry. I will not be upset. The mantra rolled across her mind as she traipsed through the breezeway that her uncle had added between the garage and the house. With her uncle's help, she had also remodeled the old house and made it her own. She didn't want her sister to come in and make it a pigsty.

Opening the back door, Juliane took a deep breath and prepared for the worst. Instead, wonderful smells greeted her as she stepped into the kitchen.

Elise turned from the counter where she was preparing some kind of salad. "Hi, Jules. You're home sooner than I expected."

"Dad and I got out of the store as soon as it closed today." Hanging up her coat on the hook just inside the door, Juliane gazed around the kitchen. "What are you doing?"

"Fixing supper." Elise returned to her salad. "I thought it would be ready when you got here, but I wasn't expecting you so soon."

Juliane couldn't contain her shock. "You…you're cooking?"

Grinning, Elise continued to work. "You sound surprised."

"But you hate cooking."

"That's before I took the time to learn how."

"But Mom tried to teach us how to cook. You were never interested."

"I know, but while I was sailing around the world, I learned. They have the most fabulous cooking classes on the ships these days for the passengers who are interested. So when I had free time that coincided with the cooking demonstrations, I took advantage."

"Wow! I'm impressed."

"Wait till you taste it."

"How soon will it be ready?"

"In about fifteen minutes." Elise glanced over her shoulder. "You have time to get out of that suit and into some comfy clothes."

Smiling, Juliane shook her head. "I can't get over it. This is a treat. I'll change and be right back, so I can help you."

Elise waved her away. "Relax. I've got it all under control."

More surprises greeted Juliane as she walked through the living room. Not a single piece of luggage remained. The room was absolutely spotless—not a speck of dust anywhere. Elise had cleaned? As Juliane headed to her bedroom, she felt a surge of guilt for her mean-spirited assumptions earlier. Elise had surprised her, just as Lukas had surprised her.

After she changed into a pair of black corduroy

pants and a gray sweater, she joined Elise. "So what are you feeding me?"

"Have a seat, and you'll find out."

Juliane turned toward the round oak table and Windsor chairs in the kitchen corner. "Are you sure you don't want my help?"

"Yes. You worked all day. Now it's your time to relax." Elise opened the oven and pulled out a roasting pan.

Dumbfounded, Juliane sat at the table as Elise filled two plates with steaming food. Last night she'd been joking when she'd asked Elise what she'd done with her sister. Now Juliane was tempted to believe that some stranger occupied the kitchen. What other changes in her sister would she discover?

Juliane stared in amazement as Elise approached the table. "You made Cornish hen?"

"Yeah, with wild rice stuffing, braised carrots and green beans." She set the plates on the table, then turned back to the counter. "I've also got a little side salad, too."

"Do you want me to give thanks?" Juliane asked as Elise slipped into a chair.

"Sure, or maybe you should taste it first." Elise chuckled.

"If it tastes as good as it smells, I'm sure I'll be thankful." Juliane bowed her head and said a short prayer, then started eating. "Elise, this is too good. I think I'll let you cook every night."

"Thanks. I'll do the cooking until I start my classes."

"What day is that?"

"Next Wednesday." Elise set her fork on her plate. "Oh, I almost forgot to tell you. That guy…Lukas… he called before you got home. He said something about going to visit his grandfather and wanted to know whether you could meet afterward to work on that banquet stuff."

"Did he say I should call him?"

"Yeah, but no need. I invited him to come over." Elise grinned. "I want to meet this guy you have no interest in."

Juliane almost choked on her bite of Cornish hen. She tried to be calm. If she protested Elise would surely think something was going on. "So what time did he say he'd get here?"

"He thought around eight o'clock because that's when his grandfather starts watching his favorite TV shows." Elise smiled smugly. "So you have plenty of time to get yourself ready for his visit."

"And just exactly what is that supposed to mean?"

Elise shrugged, still smiling. "Whatever you'd like."

Juliane lowered her gaze and tackled her food. There was no point in discussing this with Elise. She'd made up her mind that Juliane had some kind of romantic interest in Lukas so it was pointless to argue. They ate in silence for several minutes.

She wouldn't think about Lukas. Instead, guilt over

the way she'd neglected to keep in touch with her sister percolated in Juliane's mind. She should have known about Elise's newfound love of cooking. She should know why Elise had decided to stop the cruising life and go back to school. Could they be close, something they hadn't been since they were little kids?

When Juliane finished eating, she picked up her plate and headed to the sink. "Thanks, Elise. The food was terrific."

"You're welcome." Elise joined her and started putting plates in the dishwasher.

While they worked together, Juliane had dozens of questions swirling around in her mind. She might as well start with an easy one. "Did you manage to get some rest today after all the cleaning and cooking?"

Elise laughed. "So you noticed, huh?"

"I did."

"Yeah, I slept in till about eleven—eight o'clock Pacific time. My body will eventually get used the Eastern time zone."

"You do look more rested today than yesterday, but you still look like you've lost too much weight."

"Don't worry about my weight. If I keep cooking like this, I'll gain it back in no time."

"Well, it isn't fair. Why is it that the people who don't need to lose weight are the ones who have no trouble doing it?"

"Are you still worrying about your weight?" Elise poured dishwasher soap into the little cup, then pressed the buttons to turn the machine on.

"Not really." Wanting to avoid Elise's pointed gaze, Juliane lowered her head and started washing the roaster pan. She hadn't worried about her weight since Elise had left town. A few inches taller than their mother, Juliane had always wondered why she'd inherited their mother's genes for shortness and their father's genes for the tendency to carry extra weight. Elise, on the other hand, had inherited their mother's slimness and their father's height.

"Good, because you shouldn't. You have nice curves. You're not built like a stick. Look at me."

Juliane looked up to see Elise holding her arms out from her sides. Laughter bubbled up inside Juliane until she couldn't control it. "We're both dissatisfied with how we look. We are pathetic."

Elise put an arm around Juliane's shoulders and nodded. "I think you're right. We are. But don't think about that now. You'd better get ready for your visitor." Elise waggled her eyebrows.

"Quit teasing me."

"Who's teasing?"

"You're trying to make this into something it isn't." Juliane was tempted to tell Elise that she was more likely to be Lukas's type than Juliane, but the words caught in her throat. Probably because she was sure they were true. She and Lukas had been spending a lot of time together, but she knew that would change once he met Elise.

The headlights of Lukas's car illuminated the big white snowflakes that fell like confetti as he drove through an older neighborhood in Kellersburg. Creeping along the snow-covered street, he finally spotted the address that Juliane's sister had given him. He maneuvered his car into the driveway of the redbrick house with the white trim. It seemed to suit Juliane.

Getting out of his car, he took in the wide porch with the white balustrade running across the front. Unable to see the walk for the snow, he tromped through the yard and onto the porch.

Lukas took a deep breath as he rang the doorbell. Stomping the snow from his shoes, he waited for someone to answer the door. Ever since he'd talked to Juliane's sister, he'd been thinking about this opportunity to see Juliane again. He couldn't help thinking about her. At the oddest moments at home, at work or even when he was visiting with his grandfather, thoughts of her would pop into this mind.

He had to admit that his eagerness to see her even outweighed his concern about meeting her sister—another person who might judge him because of his past. He took some comfort in the fact that Juliane hadn't told anyone about his past, but sisters sometimes told each other things that they didn't tell anyone else. Either way, he wanted to make a good impression, wanted all of Juliane's family to approve of him.

As he stood there worrying about his fascination with Juliane, she answered the door. "Come in, and get out of the cold. I had no idea that the snow had already accumulated so much. The wind seems to be picking up, too."

"It has. The roads are getting slick." Unexpectedly nervous, he stomped his feet again, even though he'd already dislodged all the snow.

Shaking off the imaginary snow gave him a moment to gather his thoughts and his courage. He didn't know why he suddenly needed courage to talk with Juliane. With little difficulty, he'd told her about his life two weeks ago, then again when they'd eaten at her cousin's café. Why did he run off at the mouth whenever they were alone together? Pushing his muddled thoughts aside, he proceeded into the living room, bringing a gust of frigid air with him.

As Juliane closed the door behind him, a tall, very slim young woman stepped forward. "Hi, I'm Elise, Juliane's sister. I'm the one who talked to you on the phone."

"Nice to meet you, Elise. Thanks for inviting me over.".As Lukas glanced from Elise to Juliane, their differences struck him. If he'd passed them on the street, he'd never have guessed they were sisters. Juliane resembled her cousins more than Elise.

"Is Ferd doing well tonight?" Juliane's question shook him from his thoughts.

"As ornery as ever."

"So he must be okay?"

Smiling, Lukas nodded. "He's finally getting used to his hearing aids and agreed to come to church with me on Sunday."

"I'm glad to hear things are going well for him." Juliane held out a hand. "Let me take your coat."

"Sure." Stepping farther into the room, Lukas shrugged out of his coat. When she took it, their hands accidentally touched. His heart picked up speed, and he didn't miss the look in Juliane's eyes before she turned away. Had she felt the spark, too, or was that his imagination?

As Juliane left, he tried not to think about it. He turned his focus on the room with its shining hardwood floor covered with a colorful area rug. He took in the landscape painting of a covered bridge hanging on the wall above the couch. He liked Juliane's taste. There he was again—thinking about her. Did everything push his thoughts in her direction?

"I hope you guys don't mind my listening in on your meeting." Elise made herself at home on one end of the couch.

"No problem."

Juliane returned to the room. "What's no problem?"

"For me to join in your meeting."

"That's fine." A little frown puckering her brow, Juliane motioned for him to sit in the nearby chair while she sat on the opposite end of the couch from Elise.

As Lukas sat on the chair near Juliane, he wondered what had caused her frown. Was she still reluctant to meet with him, reminiscent of that night after the first choir practice? What had changed since their last meeting? Or was Elise's presence a problem? He couldn't believe he was letting all this speculation clutter his mind.

He had to quit making conjectures and asking himself all these questions for which he had no answers. "So where do we start? What kind of entertainment do you usually have at this banquet?"

Biting her bottom lip, Juliane glanced at Elise, as if her sister could tell them what to do. "Good question."

"Don't look at me." Elise shrugged, drawing her knees to her chest and hugging her legs. "I haven't been around for six years. I'm only observing."

"What did they do last year?" Lukas asked.

Juliane shook her head. "I don't have a clue. I don't know why Val put me in charge of this. I was busy coordinating the servers in the kitchen last year."

"I know why she asked you." Elise chuckled. "She knows you can't say no."

"That's not true."

Elise shook her head. "When was the last time you said no to someone who asked you to do something?"

Juliane let out a heavy sigh, her shoulders sagging. "Okay, I guess you're right."

Lukas took in the exchange. He'd thought that he and Juliane had become friends. Was Juliane's inability to say no the only reason she'd agreed to work with him? Was that why she'd helped him with his grandfather?

Sitting forward in the chair, Lukas wondered about the wisdom of interjecting himself into this conversation. He cleared his throat. "Elise, did I hear that you used to sing on a cruise ship?"

Elise nodded. "That's what I did for nearly six years."

"There you go." Lukas held out a hand toward Elise. "Our entertainment."

"I'll be glad to help, but I can't be the entire entertainment. What would I sing—secular or religious?"

"Whatever we come up with that works, as far as I'm concerned," Juliane said.

Elise steepled her hands in front of her mouth for a moment, then lowered them. "How about…they used to do this thing on the ship sometimes where they played a game like that old TV show *The Newlywed Game*. They separate the husbands and wives and ask them questions about each other. They got points if their answers were the same. Do you think people would enjoy that?"

"You mean like have couples who attend the banquet participate? Only we wouldn't have newlyweds."

"Yeah, it works just as well with people who've been married for years."

"Oh, that sounds like fun." Juliane grabbed a pen and a tablet from the drawer in the end table that sported a chunky ceramic lamp. "I'll make a list of ideas."

"Brainstorming. No idea is too crazy to consider." Lukas settled back in his chair. Maybe this was going to work out after all. The tension he'd sensed earlier between the sisters seemed to have eased.

Juliane giggled. "I just thought of something…oh, no…on second thought, maybe not."

"Come on. What were you thinking?" Lukas would love to read her mind…or maybe he wouldn't. He didn't want to find out that she still didn't like him much and was only doing this to please her cousin or because she thought it was her Christian duty.

Shaking her head, Juliane pressed her lips together, then burst out laughing. "I'm so sorry. Forget I said anything."

"We should put all ideas on the table."

"Not this." Juliane vigorously shook her head.

"Come on, Juliane. Tell us." Elise eased her feet back onto the floor.

"Jasper Cornett does these really corny impressions."

"Write it on the list." Lukas leaned over and tapped the tablet Juliane had on the table in front of her.

"Just because we write it down, doesn't mean we have to use it."

Juliane quickly scribbled her ideas on the page. "Okay, are you satisfied?"

An hour passed as they filled the tablet page with ideas. "We've got a good start." He glanced over at Elise. "You have any other ideas?"

"Fresh out, but I've got cookies I made this afternoon. Anyone up for cookies and hot chocolate?"

"That sounds great," Lukas replied.

Elise hopped up from the couch. "You two can keep working while I get the snacks."

"You made cookies, too?" Juliane asked.

"Don't get used to it."

"Oh, I won't."

Lukas wasn't sure, but he thought he caught some kind of underlying meaning in the exchange between the sisters as Elise left. He wasn't sure what to make of the relationship between the two women. While Elise busied herself in the kitchen, Lukas and Juliane continued to toss around entertainment ideas.

A few minutes later, Elise reappeared carrying a plate of chocolate-chip cookies and a large red teapot. She set them on the dark oak coffee table in front of the couch. "I'll be back in a minute with the mugs."

After Elise returned, she filled the mugs with the hot chocolate and put a few miniature marshmallows on top. "All right. Enjoy."

"Thanks." Lukas grabbed one of the mugs. Steam swirled out of the top, and the heat from the hot chocolate radiated through the mug and warmed his hands. He glanced over at Juliane. Looking at her warmed his heart in much the same way, but he didn't have much hope that he warmed hers, even if the spark he'd seen in her eyes wasn't his imagination.

Despite their outwardly friendly interaction, he still sensed that she was keeping her distance. She was only going to let him get so close. That was probably a good thing. At least that's what he tried to tell himself. He took a gulp of hot chocolate, then glanced at Elise. "This is great."

Juliane picked up the plate and held it out to him. "Have a cookie. In fact, have several. I don't want these things around to tempt me after tonight."

"Yeah, Juliane's worried that she might gain a pound."

Even though Juliane laughed as if Elise's teasing didn't bother her, Lukas didn't miss the little hint of venom in the look she shot Elise. "I'll put some in a baggie for you to take home. All of us can't be skinny like some people I know."

"Sounds great. I love chocolate-chip cookies." Lukas took a bite and ruminated about the sibling rivalry that was obviously going on here. Being an only child, he couldn't relate. And he certainly didn't understand why Juliane would feel self-conscious about her weight. Lukas liked looking at Juliane's feminine curves rather than Elise's slim model-like figure. But then he shouldn't be thinking about Juliane's curves anyway.

Trying to focus his attention elsewhere, he picked up the list Juliane and he had compiled. "We've got a great lineup here. Anything else you ladies want to add?"

Shaking her head, Juliane looked at him over the top of her mug. "I think we've got all the entertainment we need."

While they munched on the cookies and drank the hot chocolate, they hashed out the details for the entertainment, even calling Jasper, who agreed to do his impressions. They finalized their list and decided on the order of the program.

Juliane plunked her mug on the table. "How do we pick the couples for the game?"

Lukas finished off the last of his cookie. "Maybe we should have the people who are willing to be contestants sign up when they buy their ticket for the banquet."

"That's an excellent idea. I'll put that information in the announcement for the church bulletin." Juliane wrote something on her tablet. "I'll make a note to myself so I'll remember."

"Great." Lukas grabbed another cookie, thinking he'd better be getting home, though he wasn't in any hurry to do so. "Is there anything else we need to do?"

"Yeah, we need to come up with the questions for

the game." Juliane folded the top sheet of the legal pad back as she started a new sheet. "We can make a list of questions, then put them on note cards for the moderator."

"Who are you going to get as the moderator?" Elise wadded up her napkin and tossed it on the table.

"Why don't you do it, Lukas?" Juliane looked at him.

Lukas shook his head. "They might get tired of looking at my face if I sing and moderate, too."

Elise gathered the empty mugs. "I'm going to clean up. You two can battle this out."

After Elise left the room, Lukas turned to Juliane. "You should find someone else."

"What if I can't find someone?"

"Then I'll do it." He pointed at her. "But I'll know if you don't try very hard."

Laying her head back against the couch, Juliane laughed. "You are too funny. Of course I'll try, but everyone may turn me down."

"That's what I mean. Don't take no for an answer."

"Okay, I'll make a list of people I can ask."

"You are good with the lists."

"They keep me organized." She laughed again.

He liked hearing her laughter. He liked watching her make lists. He liked seeing her smile. He was certainly messed up—maybe in a good way—unlike the years when he'd been drinking. Why after only a couple of weeks was this woman, who could tell everyone about his disreputable past, the one woman he couldn't get off his mind?

He absolutely had to leave. There was no excuse to hang around. He stood and stretched his arms above his head. "I'd better head home."

Juliane hopped up from the couch. "I'll get your coat."

"Thanks." He hated that she seemed so eager for him to go. Obviously the time they'd shared tonight meant nothing more to her than doing the job her cousin requested. He should just be thankful she wasn't shunning him instead of wishing she could be more than a friend.

When she returned with his coat, the phone rang. "Do you need to get that?"

She shook her head. "Elise will do it."

Lukas put on his coat and picked up the bag of cookies. "I wanted to say goodbye to Elise and thank her for the cookies. Do you suppose she's off the phone?"

"One way to find out."

Before Juliane reached the kitchen door, Elise came charging into the living room. "That was Mom on the phone. She said their power is out and wanted to know whether we had any."

Juliane frowned. "Did she say why they lost their power?"

"The blizzard."

"Blizzard? I thought we were only getting a little snow. When did the forecasters say we were going to have a blizzard?"

Elise shrugged. "I don't know, but Mom says they've closed some roads because of blowing snow. And the National Guard is getting the nurses for the night shift at the hospital because the roads are impassable in the outlying areas."

"What about other parts of town?" Swallowing a lump in his throat, Lukas thought about his grandfather.

"Are you thinking about Ferd?" Juliane asked.

Lukas nodded. "Do you suppose he's lost his power?"

"I'm pretty sure his area of town is on the same grid we are. Mom and Dad live a mile from town, so they are more susceptible to power outages." Juliane placed a hand on his arm. "If you call, do you think he'll still be awake?"

Her touch momentarily froze his brain. Regaining his senses, he knew it was only a comforting gesture, but just the fact that she'd chosen to touch him brightened his thoughts. "I'm worried that he won't hear the phone when I call, because he takes his hearing aids out when he goes to bed."

"That could be a problem."

"I know." Lukas sighed. "If his power is out, that means he doesn't have any heat."

"Oh, dear. I didn't think of that." Juliane bit her lower lip.

Lukas pulled his BlackBerry from his pocket. "I'll give him a call and hope he answers."

"While you do that, I'm going to see about this blizzard." Juliane headed for the front door. "We were so busy working on the banquet stuff that I forgot all about the weather."

"Me, too. I didn't know it was supposed to get this bad." Elise followed Juliane to the door.

When Juliane opened the door, a big gust of wind blew snow from the porch onto the living-room floor. She immediately slammed the door shut and turned to Lukas. "You should see the snowdrifts! You can't even see your car in the driveway."

"It's hard to believe we were so involved in planning for the banquet that we didn't hear the wind howling out there." Elise pushed the drape aside and looked out the window.

Lukas finished his call and shoved his BlackBerry into his pants pocket. "Everything's okay. He was still awake and watching one of his shows."

"That's good news." Juliane tried to wipe up the snow with the napkins that had been on the coffee table.

"So it's bad out there?" Lukas zipped up his coat.

"See for yourself," Juliane said.

Lukas opened the door a few inches. He stuck his head out and looked at the drifts that had formed around his car, making it look like a giant marshmallow. Drifts covered the porch. He closed the door and turned around. Rubbing the back of his neck, he narrowed his gaze as he looked at Juliane. "Do you guys have a snow shovel?"

"Yeah, it's in the garage." Juliane pointed toward the back of the house.

"I only live a couple of miles away. If you get me that shovel, I should be able to dig my car out and get home. I'd feel better if I was home and close to Grandpa in case we all lose power."

"Sure. Let me grab my coat, and I'll get it for you." Juliane started toward the back door.

"You guys are crazy. Even if Lukas does dig his car out, he won't be able to see to drive home. Take another look out that window." Elise stepped over to the door. "Or better yet, go out to the street and take a look."

"Elise, if he wants to dig his car out, let him. He's concerned about Ferd."

Elise flung her arms into the air. "Okay. But I still think there's no digging out of this mess."

Again Lukas took in the sisters' conversation. Although he was disappointed that Juliane was so eager to send him on his way, he didn't want her to feel uncomfortable with him here. At the same time, he felt caught in the middle of their disagreement and worried about his grandfather's safety. "At least let me try."

"Follow me, and I'll get that shovel." Juliane headed toward the kitchen.

His spirits sank, but he charged after her. Even though he knew deep inside that she was still keeping him at a distance, he'd foolishly hoped the times they'd spent together lately had changed her opinion of him. He'd told himself her touch had meant nothing significant, so this episode should convince him that his first instincts were correct. She'd rather not have him around. When was he going to get the message?

When Juliane opened the back door a gust of wind threatened to blow it shut. Lukas reached over her head and held it open.

She glanced up at him. "Thanks."

"You're welcome."

One word of gratitude from her took his breath away. She had him swirling in the wind like the snow. Forcing his mind to think about the task at hand, he helped her open the door to the garage. She flipped the switch just inside the door. The lone lightbulb in the middle of the ceiling cast a dull yellowish light in the single-car garage that housed Juliane's little blue subcompact.

"The snow shovel is right over there." She pointed to the far wall. "Do you see it?"

"Yeah." He walked over and took it off the hook.

"I wish we had more than one. Then I could help you."

"That's okay. No sense in anyone else going out

in this storm." Lukas put on his gloves, pulled up the coat collar around his neck and picked up the shovel. "I'm ready to tackle that mountain of snow."

"Let me know if you need anything." She scurried back into the house.

Lukas trudged out into the storm, thinking that what he needed was Juliane's acceptance. Would that ever happen? Even though she seemed to understand the struggles he'd been through and seemed to believe he'd changed, for some reason she kept him at arm's length. Was it still his past or something else?

He scooped his way to his car, his mind filled with thoughts of Juliane. With each shovelful of snow, he thought of one more reason he should bury his interest in her. Why did he keep punishing himself by trying to figure out what made her tick?

Despite the cold, he was working up a sweat under his coat, but his feet were freezing. He sure could use a good pair of boots. The wind howled around him, and the blowing snow stung his face and eyes. Straightening, he arched his back to get rid of the kinks caused by the constant bending.

When he turned to look back at the garage, he could barely see the path he'd shoveled. The snow was coming down so hard visibility was limited, and the wind was drifting the snow back across the path. Was he fighting a losing battle—with the snow and with his efforts to keep from falling for Juliane?

Chapter Eight

The wind continued to howl, and Juliane kept looking out the front window as Lukas battled against the blowing snow. The front porch light barely illuminated the area enough to see him. He appeared to be a dark figure all but lost in a cloud of white. She didn't want to admit that Elise was right, but she didn't have a choice.

Juliane turned from the window and stared at her sister. "I can't let him keep shoveling that snow. He's going to freeze."

"Finally, you're convinced that this is a losing battle." Elise grabbed hold of Juliane's arm. "Lukas is stuck here. He's going to have to spend the night."

That's what I was afraid of. Thankfully she hadn't let the phrase slip out of her mouth. She didn't want Elise to know what she was feeling. Not even for an instant did she want Elise to think she had an interest in Lukas, other than keeping the poor man from freezing to death, because she didn't. Anyway, now that Elise had met Lukas, she'd clearly see that the man was out of Juliane's league, and hopefully the teasing would stop.

Juliane glanced at the door. "I guess I'll have to go out and get him."

"And apologize for letting him go out in that storm."

"He insisted. He's a grown-up. I never forced him to go."

Elise gave her an annoyed look. "Really, Juliane, did you think he was going to invite himself to stay?"

"Well—"

"Quit trying to make excuses."

"I have to get my coat first."

"Then go get it."

Juliane left before she said something she would regret. As she retrieved her coat, she couldn't believe they'd been so wrapped up in their planning that they hadn't noticed the wind howling outside. Lukas could have left earlier, but now it was too late. He was never going to dig himself out tonight.

Juliane managed to smile as she returned to the living room. She tried to ignore Elise's smug expression as she opened the door and stepped out onto the porch.

Juliane cupped her hands around her mouth. "Lukas! Lukas, quit shoveling and come into the house." The wind blew the words right out of her mouth and left her gasping for breath. She called his name again, but he still kept shoveling. With the wind howling, he probably couldn't hear. She had to go out to him.

Pulling the hood on her coat tight around her neck and face, she trudged through the snowbank. She kept her head down in order to keep the wind-driven snow from pelting her face. As she came up behind him, she called his name again. He jerked around, startling her and nearly causing her to lose her footing in the slippery snow. She grabbed hold of his arm to steady herself, and he held her up.

When she looked into his eyes, she swallowed hard while her pulse raced. She almost slipped again. "You've got to come in. You're going to freeze out here."

"But I'll never get home if I do." He pointed to the driveway between his car and the garage. "The snow is already covering what I've shoveled."

Juliane nodded. "That's my whole point. You'll never dig your car out until it quits snowing and blowing. I know you're worried about your grandpa, but please come into the house."

Lucas looked ready to argue, but finally nodded his agreement. "What do you want me to do with the shovel?"

"Just put it on the porch." Understanding Lukas's

frustration, Juliane turned toward the house and trudged back through the snow.

Without another word Lukas followed. She knew she had to apologize, and she didn't want to do it in front of Elise.

When they reached the porch, she turned. "Lukas, I'm sorry I ever let you come out here. I should have invited you to stay from the beginning."

"All that work for nothing." He looked back at the driveway and shook his head. "I'll have to do it all over again in the morning."

She grimaced. "I'm so, so sorry. You won't have to do this again. I'll have Dad send over the guy who plows out his driveway. He'll get you out."

"I don't know how with my car still sitting there." Lukas smiled wryly. "And you don't have to keep apologizing. You didn't force me to try to dig out my car. I'll have to pray that Grandpa doesn't lose his power."

"I'll pray, too, but I feel terrible that you've been working out here for nothing." With Lukas's smile making her heart lighter, she opened the door, then turned back to him. "Don't worry about wiping your feet."

"I'm not sure I can even feel my feet." He slipped out of his shoes as soon as he stepped inside.

"Well, if it isn't the Abominable Snowman." Elise carried a dustpan and broom. "I'll sweep up the snow. You guys get out of your coats."

"Do I look that bad?" Lukas chuckled.

"Not bad, just snowy."

"Let's go into the kitchen. We can take off our coats and brush all the snow off in there." Juliane hated that she was jealous of the way Elise could joke around with Lukas. She knew she didn't have any business feeling that way for so many reasons—the most important being that she was determined to have no personal interest in him.

When they reached the kitchen, Juliane took off her coat and shook it, creating a mini snowstorm. She glanced over at Lukas, who was doing the same. His dark hair dampened by the snow, he looked more handsome than ever. Her heart melted into a puddle like the snow on her kitchen floor.

Some of the unmelted flakes in his hair sparkled in the light from the florescent fixture over the stove. Tempted to reach up and brush them away, Juliane swallowed hard. She turned away to keep from acting on the impulse.

She didn't want to like this man. The idea of falling for him scared her silly. She wasn't sure she wanted him under her roof for the night, especially with Elise, even if her sister was acting as a buffer. Having him here would only add to her confusion, but she didn't have a choice.

Trying to put her thoughts on a different track, she grabbed a mop from the pantry and started to wipe up the melted snow. If only she could wipe images of Lukas from her mind as easily as she wiped up the little puddles.

Lukas reached for the mop. "Let me do that. I made most of the mess."

"No, you should get out of those wet clothes before you catch cold or something." Hoping to avoid any accidental contact, Juliane jerked the mop off to the side before he could take it.

Looking down he pointed at his feet. "You mean these soaked pants and socks?"

"Yeah."

"I'd be glad to change, but what would I put on after I do that?" A question painted his features as he eyed her.

"Hold on." Juliane laid the mop against the kitchen counter and headed out to the breezeway. Opening the door, she braced herself against the wind. "I think I have something—"

"That'll fit me?" Lukas stuck his head out the door.

"Yes. Wait inside, and I'll check this storage bin."

"Okay." He closed the door.

Shivering, Juliane lifted the lid of the bin and started rummaging through its contents. In a minute she returned to the kitchen in triumph, holding up a pair of men's sweatpants. "See. I was pretty sure these were still in there."

"Great."

"They look like they should fit." Taking in his expression, she tossed the pants to him. Was he wondering how she happened to have a pair of men's sweatpants, or was she reading something into his look that wasn't there? Should she explain?

"What are you two doing?" Elise wandered into the kitchen as a big gust of wind rattled the kitchen window.

"Finding something for Lukas to put on so he can get out of his wet clothes." Juliane pointed to the sweatpants.

"Where'd you get those?" Elise wrinkled her brow.

"Uncle Dave left them here when he worked on my house." Juliane watched Lukas to see his reaction, but his expression didn't change. She was being stupid. He didn't care why she had the sweatpants.

"So where would you suggest I change?"

"Elise, show him where the bathroom is, and I'll finish mopping up in here." Juliane watched them leave the room, hoping to regain her equilibrium before either of them returned.

Once again she'd failed to push aside all the emotions being around Lukas evoked. She couldn't rid herself of the same jittery feeling in the middle of her chest that she'd experienced when he'd handed her his coat earlier tonight.

What was she thinking—that he might be jealous because he thought those sweatpants belonged to a boyfriend? She scrubbed at the floor, wishing she could scrub all ridiculous thoughts about Lukas from her mind. Then she stopped and leaned on the mop. Where was she putting God in all of this?

Too many times lately, she'd left God out of the picture. Even after she'd told Lukas she would pray for his grandfather, she hadn't done so. She bowed her head. *Lord, please forgive me and keep Ferd safe in the storm. Help me to rely on You.*

Juliane looked up as Elise reappeared. "Is Lukas changing?"

"Yeah. Where are you planning to have him sleep?"

Juliane released a harsh breath. "That love seat in my office pulls out into a bed. I can make that up. What do you think?"

"Sounds okay to me as long as I'm not the one sleeping on the pullout bed." Elise grinned.

"Well, he could sleep on the couch in the living room."

Elise came over and put a hand on Juliane's shoulder. "I was only kidding, Jules. The pullout is fine. Guys aren't fussy."

"If you say so."

"I even found an extra large T-shirt in my things. I gave that to him as well as a pair of those airline slippers that are one size fits all. I also told him to take a hot shower. I thought that might thaw him out."

"I'm glad I put you in charge."

"Thanks." Elise picked up a couple of leftover

cookies. She bit into one and held the other one out to Juliane. "Here, have another cookie."

"No, thanks. I told you I don't need any more." Juliane put her hands on her hips. "And you didn't need to point out the fact that I'm on the plump side."

"When did I say you were plump?"

"You told Lukas I was watching my weight."

"But I never used the words *plump* or *fat*. Besides, you're the one who brought it up."

"No, I didn't. I only said I didn't want the cookies around."

"Okay. I won't mention anything remotely related to your eating habits or your weight again." Elise held her hands up in surrender. "But it seems to me that you wouldn't be so upset about the whole conversation if you didn't have your eye on Lukas."

"Not that again. Please don't mention that, either."

"You really should put me in charge of your love life."

Juliane sighed. "Oh, please."

"I'd be glad to do it."

Juliane grabbed the dish towel off the nearby rack and swung it at Elise. "I'm serious, Elise."

"Serious about Lukas? I can understand why. He's a fine-looking man."

Juliane swatted Elise with the towel again. "Quit teasing. I'm not interested."

"Okay. I'll quit teasing, but I have a serious suggestion. You should invite Lukas to go to my party with you."

"Why do you keep trying to push us together?"

"Because I think you're attracted to him, even if you deny it."

Juliane drummed her fingers on the kitchen counter as she tried to think of some kind of comeback. "You invite him."

"Not me. I'm through with men."

Juliane's eyebrows shot up. Elise was through with men? Since when? "Then why are you trying to foist him off on me? I might have the same feelings as you."

"Okay. Whatever you say."

Juliane knew Elise's verbal agreement meant nothing. She was only placating her. Juliane was fairly certain Lukas would wind up at the party no matter what she said. She might as well prepare herself for it. But for now, it was time to turn the conversation back onto Elise.

"What about the guy you were dating when Mom, Dad and I took that cruise?"

"You mean Seth?"

"Yeah, that's the one."

"History. The main reason I'm down on men. Period."

"So if you're down on men, why are you pushing Lukas at me?"

"Because, dear sister, I see how you look at him."

"And how is that?"

"You are…I don't know how to describe it exactly…maybe moonstruck."

"If I appear to be that way, I have my reasons. What do I have to do to prove to you that you're all wrong?"

"Nothing. Time will tell."

"Don't be so smug. I'm going to prove you wrong." Even as the words rolled out of her mouth, Juliane knew she might have a hard time doing it. "I don't want to argue about this anymore. Besides, what would Lukas think if he heard us?"

"He might think—"

"Don't say it." Juliane walked toward the living room. "I'm going to make up that pullout bed, then I'm going to bed myself. You can let Lukas know where he should sleep."

"And where is that?"

Putting her hand over her heart, Juliane turned at the sound of Lukas's voice. That jittery feeling hit her again, and she couldn't speak.

"In the study." Elise walked past Juliane, then turned and gave her another smug little smile. "She'll show you where that is. Good night, you guys. I'll see you in the morning."

Staring at her sister, Juliane wanted to run after Elise and quietly plead for her to take care of Lukas, but Juliane knew that would be a futile request. Instead, she turned and tried to smile as she looked at Lukas, who was now clad in the gray sweatpants, a T-shirt proclaiming the wonders of Hawaii and ugly navy-blue airline slipper socks. Even in the crazy clothes he looked good.

"So do you approve?"

Juliane's stomach did a flip-flop as she realized she'd been staring. "I guess they're better than your wet clothes."

"Hey, do you suppose I can throw my dirty stuff in your washing machine?"

Her heart racing, she went over to the set of bifold doors that hid the washer and dryer. This might be her chance to escape. "Everything you need is right behind these doors. Help yourself."

"Thanks."

"I'll go make up the pullout bed for you."

"Hey, don't go to any bother. If you lay out the bedding, I can do it myself."

"What kind of hostess would I be if I didn't do it?"

"You don't have to worry about being a hostess for me. Unexpected guests should fend for themselves."

Juliane shook her head. "Not in the household where I grew up. No one was ever made to feel unwelcome."

When Juliane headed for her office, Lukas fell into step beside her. "I hope my messing around won't keep you up. Besides the wash, I have to make some calls concerning the plant. I imagine everything in town has ground to a halt because of the storm."

"You're right." Juliane sighed, thinking about what this storm meant for the store—probably another lost day of business. "Do whatever you have to do. I'll have to call my dad to see what his plans are for the store, but I'll do it in the morning. My folks go to bed pretty early."

"So are you an early riser?" Lukas stopped in the doorway to the bathroom where a wad of clothes lay on the floor. He stooped to pick them up.

"Yeah, and Elise isn't, but don't worry about it. Do whatever you have to do tonight or in the morning." Waving a hand in the air, Juliane tried not to let Lukas's nearness in the close confines of the hallway suddenly make her want to run. "You can't be any noisier than this wind."

"Okay, then. I'll see you in the morning." Lukas started down the hall toward the kitchen.

"I'll make up your bed and leave the light on."

He stopped and turned around. "You mean like that motel commercial?"

Juliane couldn't help smiling, and his joke lightened her heart. "Not quite. We don't charge our overnight guests."

"Thanks. Hey, before I do my wash I want to run something by you. I meant to do this earlier, but with all this storm business I forgot."

"Sure. Go ahead."

"I'd like to meet early before choir practice on

Wednesday and go over that duet we're singing. Can you make it by six-thirty?"

Juliane's stomach churned at the thought of meeting Lukas alone, even if it was at church. But she had to quit being jumpy whenever they made plans to spend time together. She didn't have any store meetings to prevent her from getting there early, so she should meet him.

"If you can't make it, I understand," he said before she could respond.

She nodded. "I can make it. I had to think through my schedule."

"Great." Smiling, he turned toward the kitchen. "Good night. See you in the morning."

"Good night." She opened the door to the hallway linen closet and quickly found some bedding.

She scurried to her office and made the bed as quickly as she could. She didn't want Lukas showing up before she had finished.

Tucking in the blanket at the bottom of the bed, she realized how her old impressions of Lukas had given way to new ones. She never would have felt safe with the old Lukas Frey staying in her home, but she had no qualms about the new one...other than to wish those unaccountable fluttery feelings he seemed to stir in her would go away.

As she hurried to her bedroom, she struggled with the confusion and uncertainty in her heart.

Listening to the wind outside, Juliane sat on the edge of her bed and looked at her Bible on the nightstand. She picked it up and rubbed her hand across the smooth leather. This was what was missing in her life right now. She'd prayed earlier, but it seemed as though her prayers were getting blown away with the blizzard. Right after she'd prayed she'd managed to have an argument with Elise.

She let her Bible fall open in her lap. She glanced down at the page from a chapter in First John. Her eyes fell on the ninth verse of the first chapter. "If we confess our sins, he is faithful and just and will forgive us our sins and purify us from all unrighteousness."

Why wasn't she letting God help her deal with her mixed-up feelings about Lukas? She had to ask for forgiveness again as the verses said. She bowed her head and whispered, "Lord, forgive me for leaving You out of my life today. Please help me understand my feelings for Lukas. Help me with my relationship with Elise. And help me to remember we are all saved by Your grace. Amen."

As she laid her head on the pillow, she vowed to do two things. Make every effort to get along with her sister, and invite Lukas to Elise's welcome home party.

Chapter Nine

While Lukas sat in Juliane's kitchen and waited for his wash to get done, he punched in his grandfather's phone number. He listened as the phone rang and rang and rang. Just when he was about to end the call, his grandfather answered.

"Grandpa, it's Lukas. How are you doing?"

"I'd be doing better if you didn't keep calling and bothering me while I'm trying to watch my shows."

"I had to make sure you were okay. Why didn't your answering machine pick up?"

"Oh, it quit working a couple of weeks ago, and I didn't know how to fix it. And when I had to go to the hospital, I forgot to tell you about it."

"I'll look at it when I get a chance."

"Why are you calling so late?"

"I called to tell you I'm still at Juliane's place because I couldn't dig my car out of the snowdrifts.

I'm stuck here, and Juliane is letting me sleep on her pullout bed tonight. Hopefully I'll be able to dig out in the morning."

"I guess if I could not get you two together, God could do it with a snowstorm." Ferd chortled.

Shaking his head, Lukas ran a hand through his hair. Should he even bother trying to refute his grandfather's claim? "Grandpa, you know God didn't send a snowstorm to push Juliane and me together."

"You can't know all the ways of God."

"Well, neither can you." Lukas sighed. "I wanted you to know that I wasn't home. If you need me for anything or for any reason, you can call me on my mobile phone. You got that?"

"Yes, I do."

"Good. And don't get any crazy ideas about trying to shovel your walks or driveway. If I can't do it, I'll hire someone to do it."

"Don't worry about me. I'm doing fine."

"Okay, Grandpa. Good night." Ending the call, Lukas wished he didn't have to worry about his grandfather, but Lukas never knew what the older man might do.

Lukas stared at his BlackBerry. He had to touch base with his assistant manager Tim Drake. They were probably going to be short on workers tomorrow because of the storm, if any of them could get there at all. Downtime at the plant meant getting behind on orders. Could they make up the lost time? Another worry he had to add to the list. He was grateful for Tim, who was a great manager and a good friend, but there was only so much either of them could do in this weather.

The whir of the spin cycle on the washer stopped. Thankful for something to take his mind off his problems, even for a moment, Lukas hopped up and put the clothes in the dryer. In the past, mounting worries like these would've had him downing a six-pack of beer—sometimes more. Grandpa may not have been right about the storm forcing him to spend time with Juliane, but being here to ride it out put Lukas in a place where he couldn't give in to the temptation to find a drink somewhere. He thanked God for that.

Lukas couldn't let his current problems tempt him to throw away six years of sobriety. He had to remind himself that, despite his worries, his life was looking pretty good right now. He had a good job. He was making new friends. Grandpa was on the mend. Lukas couldn't let Bill Martin down, or God, who had brought him out of the wilderness of alcoholism.

And Lukas intended to prove to Juliane, and to himself, that he was a changed man.

Lukas paced the floor while he made a few more calls about the plant. He and his assistant manager made some contingency plans that covered all scenarios. This kind of thing was a true test of his management skills. He had a lot of people to please, and he wanted to do it right.

Finally, the buzzer sounded on the dryer. Glad to call it a night, he plodded back to Juliane's office with his pile of folded laundry. He laid it on the desk chair, turned off the light and slipped into bed.

But sleep wouldn't come. He tossed and turned on the pullout bed. The bed wasn't his problem. His mind was. He couldn't shut down his brain and go to sleep. The whistling wind and rattling windows in the old house didn't help, either. His thoughts tumbled around work, his grandfather and Juliane. All that time to think while he'd been waiting for his laundry had his mind too keyed up to sleep now.

Giving up any hope of falling asleep, Lukas turned on the light. He glanced around the room. A bookcase stood in one corner. What would he find there? Maybe something he could read to take his mind off the things that prevented him from sleeping. He perused the titles and saw a lot of books related to business, dealing with people and Bible study guides. Juliane's reading choices appeared to be all about serious subjects.

Then he spied a small paperback book tucked in between two hardcover books. He pulled the little paperback off the shelf and looked at it. A banner across the top read, "Heartwarming Inspirational Romance."

Maybe Juliane wasn't all business. Did this little romance novel mean she had a lighter side? He let his thumb fan the pages.

When his thumb stopped on a page near the front, he wondered what he would find inside a romance novel. He opened up the page and started to read the lone paragraph at the top that turned out to be two verses from the Thirty-second Psalm. He read them out loud. "You are my hiding place; you will protect me from trouble and surround me with songs of deliverance. I will instruct you and teach you in the way you should go; I will counsel you and watch over you."

Lukas let the words filter through his mind. Was this God's message to him tonight? What kind of a romance novel contained scripture? His curiosity prompted him to start reading.

Three hours later he closed the book. Sleepy eyed, he pushed the book back into its place on the shelf. The little paperback's message of love and redemption spoke to him more than he wanted to admit.

The next morning Lukas awakened with a start. Where was he? Then he remembered. Juliane's house. Jumping out of bed, he snatched his BlackBerry off the desk and looked at the time. Only eight o'clock. Thankfully he hadn't slept till noon after reading until three in the morning. He glanced at the little book that had kept him up too late last night. Wouldn't the guys at work have a good time ribbing him if he told them he'd been reading a romance novel?

Light flooded around the miniblinds on the sole window in the office. Eerie quietness indicated the end of the storm. He opened the blinds. Although whiteness greeted him as far as he could see, the snow had stopped. He wondered whether the leaden sky indicated more storms on the horizon but there was no time for speculation now. Despite his lack of sleep, he was ready to dig his car out of the drifts and get to the plant.

First, he had to call his grandfather. Picking up his BlackBerry, he sat on the edge of the bed. He listened to the ringing on the other end and prayed that Grandpa would hear the phone. On the seventh ring, his grandfather answered.

"Hi, Grandpa. How are you this morning? Did you survive the storm?"

"Well, I am answering the phone, am I not?"

"You are. So you must be okay."

"Doing great. Are you still at Juliane's?"

"Yes."

"How soon will you get home?"

"I don't know. I have to dig my car out. Then I need to check the plant, but I can come by your place first if you need me."

"No. That is all right. I am getting along fine. You take care of your business."

"Okay, I'll see you later." Ending the call, Lukas wondered how much truth there was behind his grandfather's I'm-okay routine. Right now Lukas had to believe what the older man said. Worrying about it wasn't going to change a thing.

Then Lukas called his assistant manager to make sure the plans they'd made the night before were still in place. After a brief reassuring conversation, Lukas grabbed his clothes and hurried into the bathroom. He looked in the mirror. Bloodshot eyes stared back at him. He rubbed the dark stubble on his chin. The image reminded him of the way he'd often looked when he'd had too much to drink the night before. He thanked God that wasn't the case this morning.

He started to change but thought better of it and stayed in the sweatpants. There was no sense in getting his good clothes soaked again while he tried to dig out. Maybe when he finished that task, he might get a razor in order to shave. Right now all he wanted was a toothbrush. He hoped Juliane had an extra one lying around.

As he approached the kitchen the smell of brewing coffee wafted his way. He poked his head around the corner. Juliane and Elise sat at the kitchen table while they ate without talking. A small television on the kitchen counter broadcast the morning news anchor's reports on the aftermath of the storm. "Good morning."

Elise looked up first. "Well, Mr. Sleepyhead has decided to show his face."

"Good morning, Lukas." Juliane's rather subdued greeting made him remember what he must look like.

He rubbed the stubble on his chin. "Yeah…well, I didn't intend to sleep in, but I tossed and—"

"I shouldn't have made you sleep on the pullout bed," Juliane interrupted as she placed a hand over her heart. "I feel terrible that you didn't get any sleep."

"It wasn't the bed as much as the storm. All that howling wind." Smiling, Lukas shook his head. He certainly didn't want to confess that his anxiety had resulted in his spending half the night reading one of her romances.

"Have some breakfast with us." Juliane hopped up and went to the cupboard. "We have oatmeal, but if you don't like that I have cold cereal."

"Oatmeal is fine, but before I eat I'm in need of some toiletries—toothbrush, razor. I don't know if you can help me out, but—"

"Oh, sure. I'll see what I can do." Juliane rushed from the kitchen.

Lukas turned around and looked at Elise. "Is she always this hyper in the mornings?"

Chuckling, Elise shrugged. "I've been gone for six years, so I don't have a clue."

"Oh, right."

"My guess would be yes."

"I'm going to see what she's come up with." Lukas wandered back toward the room where he'd slept.

Turning down the hall, he saw Juliane going into the office. He entered behind her as she set a brand-new toothbrush, a woman's razor and a can of ladies' shaving gel on her desk. She turned to go and ran into him.

He caught her by the shoulders with both of his hands. When she looked up, he could have sworn just for a second he saw panic in her eyes. "Whoa. I didn't mean to scare you."

She lowered her eyes as he dropped his hands. She stepped aside so he could enter and darted into the hall. Looking back through the doorway, she grimaced. "Sorry about the ladies' shave gel and razor."

Picking up the shave gel, he studied the label and chuckled. "I hope the guys at work don't get a whiff of me smelling like a fruity mango."

Juliane burst out laughing, then stared at him wide-eyed. "I'm sorry, but that struck me funny."

"No need to be sorry." Lukas enjoyed hearing her laughter. What would it be like to hear that sound every morning? His mind froze. He needed to stop thinking like that. Her close proximity, mixed with the snippets of the romance novel that floated through his mind, had him thinking things that threatened to derail his plan to concentrate on his grandfather and his job.

"While you get ready, I'll fix your bowl of oatmeal."

"Thanks," he called after her as she scurried away.

A few minutes later, Lukas joined the two women at the kitchen table. He dug into his oatmeal and hoped he wouldn't have any more crazy thoughts about Juliane. The news station from Cincinnati continued to report on the results of the storm. Lukas watched the reporter who stood next to a snowdrift that dwarfed her.

"Wow! I hope the drift my car is buried under isn't as big as that." Lukas turned to Juliane. "Have you been outside?"

"No. I tried to get out the front door, but it's frozen shut. I couldn't make it budge. And the breezeway is full of drifts just past the storage bin. I wasn't going to tromp through those."

"As soon as I finish this, I'll see if I can get that front door open." Lukas ate a spoonful of oatmeal.

Elise pointed toward the living room. "I looked out the window. I couldn't even see your car."

"Have you talked with your parents? Did they get their power back?"

"I talked to Dad this morning. No power yet." Juliane got up and put her bowl in the dishwasher.

"How did they survive without any heat?" Lukas took another bite.

"Thankfully they have a fireplace insert and lots of wood. Mom said they slept in the family room to keep warm."

"I remember doing that when we were kids." Elise

joined Juliane in front of the dishwasher. "Do you remember the time when the pipes burst and it took almost a week before someone could fix them?"

"Yeah, we had to buy drinking water and took our showers at Uncle Dave's house."

While Lukas finished his breakfast, he listened to the two sisters reminisce about past storms. He envied their camaraderie. What would his life have been like if he'd had a brother to share it with, or even a sister? He had to admit that he'd been a lonely child, feeling out of place even in his own family. Much of that had been his own fault.

After reconnecting with his grandfather, Lukas realized he wanted a family life. Although his grandfather was sometimes cantankerous, Lukas enjoyed being with him.

He saw this with Juliane and Elise. They might not always agree, but he could tell they loved each other. Even now, when he was getting vibes that some unspoken disagreement was floating between them. Elise's expression told him that she was trying to get Juliane to do something she didn't want to do. Did it have something to do with him, or was he being paranoid?

Shaking the speculations away, he finished eating. After putting his bowl in the dishwasher, he took his coat from the hook by the back door, then glanced around. "Do you know where my shoes are?"

"Don't worry about your shoes. I found something for you earlier this morning in the storage bin." Juliane raced out the back door and returned, holding up a pair of big black rubber boots. "I hope these will fit you."

"Even if they don't, I'll wear them. They'll work better than my shoes." Lukas sat on one of the kitchen chairs and pulled the boots on. "They're a little big, but they'll do."

With Juliane and Elise behind him, Lukas clomped to the front door. "Let's see if I can get this door open."

Juliane peered out the front window. "I think there's a big drift right in front of it. That's why I couldn't get it open."

Turning the doorknob, Lukas pushed the door with his shoulder. He hoped the door would open because he didn't want to look like a wimp in front of Juliane. As he pushed harder, he felt movement. With a powerful shove, he managed to open the door, pushing aside the frozen mound of snow in front of it.

He turned in triumph. When Juliane smiled and applauded, his heart soared. How pathetic was he that he wanted her accolades? He wanted to be a hero in her eyes, not the drunk that she remembered.

"Okay. I'm off to dig out my car." He squeezed out the opening between the door frame and the door.

Juliane stuck her head through the narrow opening. "Oh, I forgot to tell you that Dad is going to bring us the snowblower after they get out. He said that would work to clear the driveway, since we can't have it plowed because your car's in the way."

"Great." Lukas heard the door close as he trudged over to the snow shovel that still sat against the front of the house.

Shoveling a path to his car, he wondered how much progress he would make before Juliane's dad arrived with the snowblower. While Lukas worked, images of Juliane invaded his thoughts. Every time she came unbidden to his mind the story line of that romance novel came along, too. He couldn't let himself think of Juliane in the context of romance, could he?

For days, he'd been fighting those very thoughts. Spending this time with Juliane and her sister had made him wish for a family. He had worked on becoming Juliane's friend, but he wanted more than friendship. His wish for family included her. There, he'd admitted it, but would she consider taking a chance on him? Could he make that happen? Despite all his efforts not to let himself want something he couldn't have, he was falling for Juliane.

Juliane removed the scarf from around her neck and drank in the warmth of the church foyer. Opening one of the double doors leading into the sanctuary, she let out a deep sigh. She hoped by arriving a half an hour early for her meeting with Lukas that she would have time to prepare herself. The quiet sanctuary afforded the perfect place to pray. Trying to figure out her mixed-up feelings about him required a lot of prayer.

Lukas had been on her mind at every turn, and she'd stewed about this meeting since he'd requested it two days ago. She still had to fulfill her promise to herself to invite Lukas to Elise's party. Tonight was the night to issue that invitation. She wouldn't chicken out.

Sliding into the back pew, she looked up at the cross that hung high on the wall at the back of the stage, illuminated by a lone spotlight. Darkness filled the rest of the room. A sense of calm surrounded her as she bowed her head. She closed her eyes and absorbed the quiet as it settled into her soul. *Be still before the Lord.* The words from one of the Psalms echoed through her mind.

As she let God's peace fill her heart, someone started strumming a guitar. She looked up. A man sat in the shadows on one side of the choir loft, his head lowered as his fingers moved across the strings. He raised his head slightly, and she caught a glimpse of his face. Her heart raced when she realized the man was Lukas.

He must have entered from one of the side doors. He clearly had no idea she was here. Should she say something? Before she could open her mouth, he began to sing. His marvelous tenor voice rang out over the empty pews. He wasn't singing one of the songs that the choir was doing for the Winter Festival, but as he sang, she recognized the contemporary Christian tune she'd heard on the radio. She listened as raw emotion poured out of his voice.

The words of the song about never being alone washed over her, filling her heart with God's love. Lukas sang the lyrics as one who had experienced the pain and heartache of being alone and how God had reached down and let him know that he wasn't alone anymore. She remembered Lukas talking about himself as the shy and lonely teen who had started drinking to overcome his feelings of inadequacy.

Tears welled in her eyes as a pressure filled her chest. She blinked and tears rolled down her cheeks. She wiped them away with the back of her hand.

Why had she let that long-ago episode color her thoughts about this man for so long? Even as she asked herself the question, she knew her fears had been less about his past and more about the future. She'd feared Lukas would be like her father—unable to stay sober.

Her father was never a mean or abusive drunk. He was sad and maudlin when he drank. When he fell off the wagon, he'd drink himself into a stupor every night, then somehow get up the next morning and go to work. Juliane never knew what caused him to drink or what suddenly made him quit. She wanted to know, but she always followed her mother's example and didn't bring it up when he was sober. Her mother seemed to think talking about it would send him right back to drinking.

Initially, she'd feared the same thing with Lukas. But after hearing his story, she'd known that Lukas had an anchor in the Lord that her father had never found. And in his music, she could hear it. The strength of his faith warmed her and silenced her doubts. She'd prayed for peace of mind, and now she knew her prayer had been answered.

"Lukas." Even though she'd whispered, her voice sounded loud in the quiet room.

He looked up. "Juliane?"

"That was wonderful."

"Thanks. I didn't know I had an audience." Standing, he set the guitar on the pew where he'd been sitting. "How long have you been here?"

"Since before you started to sing." Juliane approached the platform where the pulpit stood in front of the choir loft.

"Why didn't you say something before?"

"I didn't know you were here until you started to play. I hated to disturb you." She joined him on the stage. "I had no idea you played the guitar, too."

Shaking his head, Lukas gave her what appeared to be an embarrassed smile. "I just mess around with the guitar when I'm singing for myself."

"Well, it sounded pretty good to me."

"Thanks." He turned and picked up a folder from the pew. "Should we get started? I've got the CD with the accompaniment."

"Are we going to use the sound booth?"

"No." Bending down, he retrieved a portable CD player from under the pew. He popped the CD into it. "I brought this to use for now. It's too much trouble to do the sound booth with only the two of us."

"You're right." Nervous energy buzzed through Juliane as she laid her coat across the back of the pew. Taking a deep breath, she picked up her music and turned to Lukas. "Okay. I'm ready."

He punched the play button on the CD player. The lilting sounds of an orchestra broke the silence. After the prelude, Lukas sang a short solo. Then Juliane responded with a solo of her own. After a short interlude, they started the duet. Even though they'd gone through this during the previous choir practice with the piano accompaniment, having the CD orchestra version added so much. Their voices rose to the vaulted ceiling and blended in perfect harmony.

When they finished, Lukas smiled. That familiar jittery feeling scrambled her insides.

"Hey, that wasn't too bad." Glancing her way, he stopped the CD. "Do you want to go through it again?"

"Sure." Maybe this time her stomach wouldn't feel as though it was on a roller-coaster ride.

They went through the song several more times.

Each time Juliane became more comfortable with the words and more comfortable singing with Lukas. She wanted the harmony their voices made to spill over into their lives. Would inviting Lukas to the party be the first step in creating that harmony? She had to make the invitation before the others arrived.

"So what do you think?" Lukas popped the CD out of the player.

"I thought it went very well."

"Me, too." Now what did she say? This was the moment. *Ask him.* The message sat in her brain, but her tongue wouldn't work. It felt like a wad of cotton in her mouth.

"I sure appreciate your dad letting me use his snowblower to clear Grandpa's driveway and mine. Did your parents get their power back?" Lukas picked up the CD player and his guitar.

"They did. How's Ferd doing?"

"Great! He even likes his new hearing aids." Lukas stepped off the stage. "I'm going to take this stuff out to my car."

She had to ask before he left. If she waited, the other choir members, including Elise, would be arriving by the time he returned. Juliane couldn't make the invitation in front of them. Her heart thudded. "Lukas, wait."

"What?" She read the curiosity in his eyes.

"You know...my parents are having a welcome-home party for Elise this Saturday right here in the church fellowship hall. I know this is really last minute, but she'd like for you to come. And you can bring Ferd, too." Did her voice sound as high and squeaky to him as it did to her? Oh, well, she'd made the invitation.

Nodding, he shifted the CD player in his hand. "Yeah. That sounds like fun. I'll have to see what Grandpa says, but I'll come, even if he doesn't. Thanks for inviting me."

"Good. Be prepared to meet all my aunts, uncles and cousins. We have a big family."

"So I'm beginning to see here at church." Lukas grinned. "Is this casual?"

"Oh, yeah. Lots of food, games and probably a little entertainment in the form of karaoke."

"Okay. I'd better get this stuff out to the car before everyone else gets here."

Juliane watched him go out the side door. She'd fulfilled one promise—to ask Lukas to the party. She was still working on the thing with Elise. That was an ongoing promise to keep. Juliane had to figure out what she was going to do with Lukas now that he'd plowed a hole in her wall of resistance and walked right through it and into her heart.

Chapter Ten

Music, laughter and conversation floated through the church fellowship hall. Along one wall a huge banner with bright red letters read, Welcome Home, Elise. Lukas stood in the doorway and surveyed the crowd. He spied Juliane across the room talking with a teenage girl he didn't know. Seeing her made his pulse pick up speed.

He took a deep breath and let it out slowly as he moved into the room. Maybe he could find his equilibrium before he greeted her. She hadn't told anyone, at least that he was aware of, about his past. But every new social occasion in this town caused that old anxiety to resurface.

This particular event meant running into Juliane's cousin Nathan. Lukas had yet to meet Nathan again, because he'd decided not to take part in the choir's

Winter Festival program. Nathan was too busy at the bank, and Lukas had managed to avoid him at church.

Lukas glanced over at his grandfather. "There's Juliane. I'm going over there."

Ferd turned to Lukas. "I didn't realize this was a date. So you finally took my advice and asked her out."

Lukas shot his grandfather an annoyed look. "Grandpa, this isn't a date. If it were, I would have brought her to the party, not just showed up. And I certainly wouldn't be dragging you along."

"Well, I am sorry you had to bring me."

Lukas blew out a harsh breath. "I didn't mean for it to come out like that. I'm glad you came with me. I want you to understand that Juliane and her sister, Elise, both invited us to this party. Please don't make any embarrassing comments about Juliane and me while we are here."

Ferd shook his finger at Lukas. "One of these days you're going to take my advice, and ask that girl out on a real date."

Lukas shook his head. "Whatever you say. Just drop it."

"Okay. Which one is the sister?"

Lukas hoped the pounding behind his forehead would subside as soon as his grandfather quit bugging him about Juliane. "The sister's name is Elise, and she's the tall one with the blond streaks in her hair."

"Very pretty girl. Maybe you'd like her better."

"I don't like her better."

"So you do like Juliane."

Lukas clamped his mouth shut and counted to ten. He was going to ignore that comment because no matter what he said, his grandfather wouldn't be convinced that there wasn't something going on with Juliane. Lukas was having a hard time convincing himself. "Let's go meet Elise."

While Lukas introduced his grandfather to Elise, Juliane joined them. Lukas watched her as she joked with his grandfather. He was enjoying the attention of two pretty women.

Lukas liked the way Juliane looked in her tan turtleneck sweater that seemed to highlight her eyes. He'd let himself like a lot of things about her, but he couldn't gauge where he stood with her. Although she was friendly, that familiar tinge of distance underscored their relationship. Even when she'd asked him to the party, she seemed on edge. Maybe he was being too impatient about the situation. Time would help him prove to her that she could trust him not to be the old Lukas Frey.

"There's my friend Dot." Ferd nodded toward the other side of the room. "I am going to go over and say hello."

"Okay, Grandpa."

Ferd looked at Juliane. "Take care of my grandson, and keep him out of trouble."

"I think you're the one they need to keep out of trouble." Juliane winked at Ferd.

"I am too old to get in trouble." Ferd winked back, then shuffled across the room.

"Did you say you knew Dot from the senior center?" Lukas asked.

"Yes, and Dot's also my aunt Ginny and uncle John's neighbor." Juliane chuckled. "And I think I see a little romance in bloom."

"I don't know about the romance, but thanks for inviting Grandpa. He was thrilled that you did."

"I thought if he got to know more people from the church, he'd feel more comfortable coming with you. Especially since you are sitting with the choir, and he would have to sit by himself."

"He's more eager to attend church now that he has adjusted to his hearing aids." Lukas contented himself with talking about his grandfather though he really wanted to know whether he had received his invitation because Juliane wanted him there. She'd never said she'd like him to attend. She'd only indicated that Elise had issued the invitation. Why did he have to be so desperate for Juliane's approval?

The evening continued with a buffet supper during which Elise's aunts, uncles and cousins took turns roasting her with funny stories from the past. But Juliane had the entire room laughing when she told them about the time that Elise opened one of her Christmas presents early, then rewrapped it and put it back under the Christmas tree. On Christmas morning she discovered that someone had replaced the gift with a comic strip about someone receiving an empty box because they had opened a gift early.

When the laughter died down, Juliane's parents stood and each told a touching story about Elise and Juliane. They raved about their daughters and thanked God for great family and friends. After they finished, applause filled the room.

Glancing at his grandfather, Lukas felt the need to thank the older man for trying to help him all those years ago, even though he hadn't listened to the advice. Maybe now wasn't the right time for that conversation, but he intended to have it on the way home.

After the tables were cleared, Juliane's dad and several others started setting up the karaoke machine. Other people were setting up board games on various tables around the room. There was a game for every taste and every age group. Lukas took in the joy that filled the room and wished he could claim a big happy family like this. He tried to soak up the cheer.

While Lukas stood there, a man about his age with sandy-brown hair, cut in an almost military style, approached Lukas. The man extended his hand. "Hi, I'm Nathan Keller. I'm not sure whether you remember me, but we worked on some theater productions together when we were in college. I read in the local paper about you becoming the manager of the medical devices plant. I want to officially welcome you to Kellersburg."

"Thanks, Nathan." Lukas's stomach churned as he shook Nathan's hand. He didn't remember Nathan. If they'd met on the street, Lukas wouldn't have known the other man. How was he going to deal with one more person who knew about his past?

"I'm vice president of the local bank, so I'm also here to help you with any of your banking needs." Nathan smiled wryly. "I had to say that. If my dad was in earshot, he'd have my head if I didn't promote the bank."

Nathan's droll comment about his banking duties put Lukas a little more at ease, but he was still trying to think of how to approach Nathan's introduction. Sometimes honesty came with a price. "When I met Juliane again, she mentioned that you worked at the bank, and she also thought we probably knew each other. But I have to be honest—I'm bad at remembering people from those years. I don't recall meeting you."

"That's okay. We only met in passing a few times. I had a couple of insignificant parts in a few plays." Nathan smiled. "Juliane told me you are singing the lead in the musical for the Winter Festival."

"I am. Did I hear that was supposed to be your part?"

"Not necessarily. As you might have noticed, there are a lot more women than men in the choir."

Lukas grinned. "I did notice the men are outnumbered."

"Anyway, whenever any special parts for men came up, I was always tapped to take it."

"Yeah, that's what Juliane told me."

"But this year I've been dealing with more work than I need at the bank." Nathan shook his head. "I couldn't fit choir practice into my schedule. I'm thankful you moved to town and took that part."

"Glad I could help." Lukas sensed an acceptance he hadn't expected from Nathan.

"I hope you like living in Kellersburg."

"So far I can't complain." Lukas breathed a sigh of relief when Nathan didn't want to reminisce about their college years.

"How did the plant weather the storm?"

"We've had people doing double shifts this week to make up the time we lost. But we're back on schedule now."

"I'm sure you're relieved to get caught up."

"Yeah, we had a couple of big orders in the pipeline. I certainly wanted to make delivery on time." Lukas couldn't help wondering what Nathan was thinking while he made small talk. Was the man trying to figure out whether Lukas was still drinking? Lucas didn't remember Nathan, but Nathan remembered him. And Juliane had indicated that Nathan remembered those problematic years. Lukas hated that those years would always haunt him.

Juliane helped finish the last of the cleanup in the kitchen. Looking through the service opening between the kitchen and the fellowship hall, she watched Lukas talking with Nathan. What were they talking about? Although they seemed to be conversing like old friends, she wondered how Nathan viewed Lukas. Could she casually join their conversation? She laid the dish towel on the counter and meandered in their direction.

As she drew closer, Nathan glanced her way. "Hey, Juliane, are you up for another Trivial Pursuit challenge? Val and Carrie are setting up the board."

"Men against the women again?"

"Absolutely. I've recruited Lukas here for the men's team." Nathan clapped Lukas on the back. "That means the women will lose again for sure."

"Don't be so smug."

"You mean the men always win?" Lukas asked.

"Always." Nathan grinned.

"That's not true." Juliane glared at Nathan.

"Okay, you're right." Nathan pretended to think. "I believe I remember you women winning one game two years ago on New Year's Eve."

Juliane decided to ignore Nathan's teasing comment. "Did you ask Elise to join the women's team?"

"Val did."

Lukas looked from Nathan to Juliane. "So this Trivial Pursuit thing is an ongoing event?"

"Yeah, whenever the family gets together, for whatever occasion, there is at least one Trivial Pursuit match going on." Juliane motioned toward the other side of the room where her dad had finished setting up the karaoke machine on a small stage. "Before we start the game, it looks like we're going to have some entertainment. Dad has to get in his karaoke."

Lukas wrinkled his brow. "Your dad sings?"

"Every time we have a family get-together. Now you know where Elise got her longing to entertain."

Nathan looked pointedly at Juliane. "I think that applies to both of his daughters."

"Maybe, but I'm hardly in the same league with Elise. My entertaining is limited to this little town."

Lukas turned from watching the preparations. "So if your dad likes to sing, why doesn't he sing in the choir?"

"Because that would require practice." Juliane laughed. "With karaoke he can just get up and sing."

"So what does he sing?" Lukas asked.

"I think that's half the fun. Nobody knows until he gets up there." Nathan motioned toward the corner of the room. "Let's grab a seat at the Trivial Pursuit table and get ready for the entertainment."

"Sure." Following Nathan, Juliane wondered what

Lukas thought about the family gathering. Did he find it enjoyable or rather odd? What difference did it make? Why should she care what he thought of her family? But in spite of herself, she did care. When it came to Lukas Frey she was starting to care very much.

After almost everyone was seated, Juliane noticed Ferd sitting with Dot. She leaned over to Lukas. "Looks like your grandfather has found a companion for the evening."

"I guess. How long has he known Dot?"

"They've both been coming to the senior center ever since I started volunteering there a couple of years ago."

"Grandpa's only lived here a couple of years. So he must've started going there as soon as he moved here." Lukas glanced over at his grandfather again. "So why do you suppose he is just now showing an interest in Dot?"

"Maybe he decided it was time."

"Yeah…" Lukas had a faraway look in his eyes as his voice trailed off.

Before Juliane could comment, her father hopped up on the stage and grabbed the microphone. "Hello, everyone. It's good to see you all tonight."

There was a smattering of applause and some shouts of agreement from several people.

Ray held up one hand. "I know you've all been waiting for this."

"What would a family gathering be without one of your songs?" someone yelled, and laughter rippled through the room.

"It'd be mighty boring." Ray gave a big belly laugh as he looked over the crowd. "We're all here to welcome Elise home, so I'm going to sing a song especially in her honor. Then we're going to get her up here to sing something. She's the professional in the family."

A little stab of jealousy pierced Juliane's heart as she listened to her father praise Elise. Juliane knew she had to get over it. She'd promised herself that she'd put away the petty jealousies, but accomplishing that task was harder than she had expected. Besides, her dad was right. Elise was the professional vocalist.

While Juliane stewed over her own lack of self-discipline, her father started to sing a song made popular by James Taylor. The words about showering the people you love with love hit Juliane's heart right where the jealousy resided and helped to push it away. When Ray finished singing, Elise ran up to the stage and flung her arms around him. Applause filled the room as father and daughter stood arm in arm to face the crowd.

"Thanks, Dad." Giving her dad a kiss on the cheek, Elise grabbed the microphone. "And thanks, everyone, for coming out tonight to welcome me home. It's so good to be here with family and friends. Now I'm going to sing a song that expresses my feelings about being home."

As Elise started to sing, Juliane closed her eyes. She let the words of the song originally sung by Tim McGraw, which told of finding a place to belong, fill her heart. She began to see that she was the fortunate one. She hadn't had to travel the world to find out where she belonged.

Elise had said she was glad to be back in Kellersburg, but Juliane hadn't realized how true it was until now. The lyrics poured straight from Elise's heart as her voice rang throughout the room. Blinking back tears, Juliane swallowed the lump in her throat. She had to help make Elise's homecoming the best.

When Elise finished singing, cheers and applause filled the room. She hugged her father again, and a huge smile appeared as she wiped tears away. "Thanks. Now Dad and I want to have a little fun. So I hope you'll join us."

Picking up a second microphone, Ray also grabbed a small bowl from a nearby stand and walked over to Elise. "We've put everyone's name in this bowl, and we're going to draw some names of people to come and sing."

"What if we can't sing?" someone at the back of the room shouted.

"There's no one in this room who can't sing. You

won't have to sing a solo. Elise is going to sing with you. If your name is drawn, you'll be escorted to the stage."

"You mean like an offer we can't refuse?" Ray's brother Carl shouted.

"You got it, brother." Grinning, Ray held the bowl out to Elise. "Go ahead and draw a name."

"Don't go pickin' my name." Carl pretended to head for the door. "You'll be sorry if you do. Even with Elise singing with me, you'll have to hand out earplugs."

Elise stuck her hand in the bowl and pulled out a folded piece of paper. Opening it, she smiled. "First on our list of entertainers is…let's hear some applause for…Hannah Albright."

Applause, whistles and cheers sounded through the room as a teenage girl with straight brown hair swinging around her shoulders made her way to the stage.

As Elise helped Hannah get ready to sing, Juliane leaned across to Val. "I have a suspicion that Dad and Elise have rigged the draw. How about you?"

"Your suspicions are justified, but let's be thankful. That way we won't have to listen to anyone who really can't sing. Like Uncle Carl." Val grinned, then covered her mouth with one hand.

Lukas looked over at Juliane with a puzzled expression. "So why do you think a fix is in?"

"Because Hannah sings in the high school chorus

and often has lead parts in the high school musicals. She even sings solos at church from time to time."

"How come she doesn't sing in the church choir?"

"Too busy. She has something going on every night of the week." Juliane turned her attention to the stage as the first notes of the intro started to play. "Let's listen."

The bouncy tune of a contemporary Christian song rang out across the room as Elise and Hannah joined in a duet worthy of any professional recording. Would Hannah follow in her older cousin's footsteps and seek a professional career, or would she find a place in her small hometown like Juliane had? She shook the speculation away. She didn't need to dwell on the what-might-have-been scenarios for her life. Why did Elise's return have to resurrect all of Juliane's self-doubts?

When Elise and Hannah finished singing, the room exploded with applause, cheering and table pounding. Then shouts for an encore echoed off the walls. Elise and Hannah found another song to sing and brought the house down again. They were a tough act to follow, but several more Keller-family relatives stepped up to the microphone and sang with Elise.

When Ray returned to the stage, Elise handed him one of the microphones. "Okay, everyone, we're going to draw one more name. Then you can all get started with your games."

Elise drew out another slip of paper and opened it. "Lukas Frey."

Juliane's heart did a little flip-flop when she heard his name. She glanced over at him. He looked back at her with a lopsided grin. "I thought this was only relatives who had to sing."

Eric clapped Lukas on the back. "You heard the man. Every person in the room had their name in the bowl."

"But I thought Juliane said the fix was in for who was chosen."

"Well, maybe it was, but you were in the fix." Eric stood and motioned for Lukas to pass. "We're ready to listen."

Everyone at the Trivial Pursuit table clapped and made teasing remarks as Lukas went to the stage except Juliane. She wondered why Elise and Dad had decided to include Lukas in their list of performers. Juliane had no doubt after seeing whose names had been called that they'd made a list beforehand.

Juliane watched Elise instruct Lukas regarding the karaoke machine, then handed him a microphone. He looked a little bewildered as well as nervous. She tried to put herself in his shoes. How would she feel if she were asked to perform on the spur of the moment in front of a bunch of people she didn't know?

Val nudged Juliane. "Lukas is being a good sport about this, isn't he?"

"Yeah."

"I guess he figured he didn't have a choice after the little speech your dad gave." Eric laughed. "We Kellers can be pretty intimidating."

"Okay, you two, quit gabbing so we can hear." Val put a finger to her lips.

Juliane straightened and looked up at the stage as the prelude to the song blared from the speakers. Elise started the song with a solo. Juliane recognized the tune. "The Heart Won't Lie." How many times had Juliane and Elise listened to their father play the rendition of that duet by Reba McEntire and Vince Gill?

As the song progressed and Lukas had his turn to sing, jealousy sprang back up in Juliane's heart like a weed that wouldn't die. Just as she'd always suspected, Elise and Lukas made beautiful music.

All the progress Juliane had made on her promise to have only good thoughts about Elise faded like the last notes of the song as Elise and Lukas took a bow. Juliane clapped and smiled along with the rest of the crowd, but inside she was fighting a losing battle with envy. The pride on Ferd's face was the only thing that lightened her heart and made her smile. Why was doing the right thing so hard?

Chapter Eleven

A dark, quiet house greeted Juliane when she came through the back door. Had Elise gone to bed as soon as Nathan brought her home from the party? Only the light over the stove shone in the otherwise darkened room. Juliane had volunteered to stay behind to help her parents clean up the fellowship hall, so everything would be ready for Sunday-morning services.

Glad she'd had an excuse not to go home with her sister, Juliane plopped her purse on the kitchen table. She sighed and wondered when she would get rid of her troublesome feelings about Elise. Just when she thought she had them conquered, they reemerged. She closed her eyes and tried to pray, but her heart wasn't right. She whispered into the darkness. "Lord, forgive me."

As Juliane stood there, she heard a baffling noise. She strained to hear. A soft, weepinglike sound slowly infiltrated the quiet. Still not certain of what she was hearing, she cocked her head and listened. Someone *was* crying.

Elise was the only one here. Why would she be crying?

Juliane crept toward the stairs that led to the second story where Elise slept. The weeping turned into sobs. Juliane's heart sank. The sound of her sister's sobs ripped through Juliane, leaving a hollow sensation in her chest.

Not sure what she would say to Elise, Juliane climbed the stairs and switched on the hall light. The door to Elise's room was closed. Juliane stared at the door and listened to the heart-wrenching cries coming from the other side.

Elise had been so happy tonight and so glad to be home. Why would she be crying now? What had happened? *Lord, You know what's troubling Elise. I'm not the best person to talk to her, but I know You can give me the words I need to say.*

Taking a deep breath, Juliane tapped lightly on the door. The weeping stopped, but Elise didn't answer. Juliane knocked again, this time louder. "Elise, what's wrong?"

"Nothing." Elise's muffled voice sounded through the door. "Just go away."

Something told Juliane that she shouldn't do as Elise requested. "Please tell me why you're crying."

"I'm fine. Go away."

Juliane put her hand around the doorknob. The cold metal against her fingers made her shiver. "I'm not going away. I'm coming in, and you're going to talk to me."

"Don't. There's nothing to say, and there's nothing you can do. Go to bed."

"But I'll never sleep, knowing you're up here crying." Juliane turned the knob and let the door swing open.

The light from the hallway cast a long beam into the room and illuminated the bed where Elise sat. Even in the dim light the tears on her cheeks sparkled. She wiped them away as she looked up at Juliane. "You don't listen very well, do you?"

"No, I never did like doing what you told me to do." Juliane strode across the room. Sitting on the bed, she put an arm around Elise's shoulders.

Without hesitation, Elise turned toward Juliane and wept on her shoulder. Holding Elise close and noticing how thin and frail she felt, Juliane let her sister cry. What could be wrong? A dozen scenarios ran through Juliane's mind. Why wouldn't she talk?

Please, Lord, I know I haven't had the best feelings toward Elise, and I'm so sorry. You're making me see what's important.

As Juliane finished her prayer, Elise pulled away

and wiped her tears. She sat there and stared straight ahead without speaking. Juliane was thankful that Elise wasn't telling her to leave. Maybe just sitting here with her was enough for right now. They sat in silence for several minutes, Elise's sniffles the only sound in the room.

Juliane reached over and took Elise's hand and squeezed it. "Are you ready to talk?"

"Do I have to?"

"Yes. I want to know what's wrong. Are you dying or something?"

"Sometimes I feel like I'm dying."

"Why do you feel that way?"

Elise reached over to her nightstand and pulled a tissue from the holder. Wiping her nose, she stared, her eyes welling with tears. She blinked, and the tears rolled down her cheeks. She grabbed another tissue and wiped them away. She took a deep, shaky breath. "I don't know where to start."

"Anywhere. Just start."

"I wish I had your life."

Dumbfounded, Juliane stared back. "You're not serious, are you?"

"Yes. You've always been the perfect one. Mom and Dad are so proud of you. Everyone looks up to you."

Juliane wasn't sure she was hearing correctly. "And you're crying about that?"

Shaking her head, Elise covered her face with her

hands. Then she looked back at Juliane. "I don't know. I told you I didn't know where to start."

Juliane knew this wasn't the time to laugh, but laughter bubbled up, and she couldn't contain it.

"You think my problems are funny? I thought you were trying to help."

"I am, but isn't it funny that you're wishing you had my life, and I'm wishing I had yours?"

"What?"

"Yes. I've been jealous that you were cruising around the world singing and performing while I was stuck here in small-town, U.S.A. Let's see which seems more exciting." Juliane held out her left hand. "Trying to please old Mrs. Hatchett with a special dress order, smiling at customers when you'd rather scream and taking inventory of stock or…" Juliane held out her right hand. "Or singing while dressed in gorgeous, thousand-dollar costumes, visiting exotic locales around the world and eating food prepared by renowned chefs. Hmm."

Elise got up from the bed and began pacing. "Yeah, all that sounds glamorous, but it can get old after a few years."

"Do we both have the grass-is-always-greener syndrome?"

"Seems that way." Elise stopped pacing and smiled halfheartedly.

"But that still doesn't explain why you're crying.

If you wanted to get away from that life, you should be happy because you're home now." Juliane patted the bed beside her. "Come sit down again and tell me what's really bothering you."

Elise shuffled to the bed and plopped down beside Juliane. They sat in silence for several minutes. Wishing she could somehow read Elise's mind and figure out her problem, Juliane resisted the urge to push her sister into talking.

Elise drew another shaky breath, then let it out with a sigh. "You know I set up that song with Lukas to make you jealous and prove that you're falling for him. The heart won't lie."

Juliane knit her eyebrows in a frown. "How did this discussion turn to me?"

"So was I right?"

"I'm not going to answer your question until you tell me what's going on with you."

"Okay." Elise appeared to be thinking, but she remained silent.

"I'm waiting."

"How do I confess to Miss Perfect?"

Guilt roiled Juliane's stomach. Her, perfect? If only Elise knew how imperfect her sister was and how she'd been harboring jealousy all these years. "Why do you keep saying I'm perfect? That's so wrong."

"That's the way you always seemed to me."

"And here I was always thinking you were the

perfect one—with your beautiful voice and your tall model's figure."

"I told you the other night how I wished I was more voluptuous like you, not tall and gangly." Laughing, Elise flung herself back on the bed with her arms over her head.

"If I was so perfect, how come all the boys liked you and not me?" Juliane narrowed her gaze. "Remember Kyle Marston?"

"Yeah, I knew you liked him, so I went after him so you couldn't have him. You had everything else— the best grades, the student council presidency and even perfect attendance—so I wasn't going to let you have him." Elise sat up, a silly grin on her face. She placed a hand on Juliane's arm. "I saved you. He was a terrible kisser."

Juliane burst into laughter. Although they'd had an abbreviated discussion of this sort when she'd complained to Elise about mentioning her weight issues, this laughter dispelled the remaining anger she harbored toward Elise.

After the laughter ceased, Juliane studied Elise. "Okay. Now that we've both confessed about our high school years, how about telling me what's really going on here? You seem to have an excellent way of turning the discussion."

"I know." Elise smiled wryly.

"What's making you sad tonight?"

Elise released a harsh breath. "Okay. Promise you won't judge me."

"Promise." As the word passed over Juliane's lips, she knew this was a test of her resolve to get along with Elise—to forgive any past wrongs.

Elise bowed her head as if she was praying before she started. Then she raised her head and looked Juliane in the eye. "I know I told you how glad I was to be home, but tonight I realized that more than ever."

"I know. I could tell by the way you sang that song."

"You could?"

"Absolutely."

Elise placed a hand over her heart. "I am glad, but I've also realized how far away from God I've strayed." Elise lowered her head again. "It brings me to tears. I want to get right with God again."

"I'm so sorry, but I'm here to help." Touching Elise's arm, Juliane recognized her own guilt before God. "Though I'm not exactly the greatest example."

"You are to me. I always wanted to be as good as my big sister."

Juliane shook her head. "Oh, Elise, don't put me on a pedestal."

"Too late."

"Well, I'm climbing down because I'm sure to fall off."

"See? You're even humble."

Using both hands, Juliane playfully swatted at Elise. "Quit. Turn your eyes on Jesus."

"Like the old hymn says."

"Yes. Put your trust in God, not me." Juliane put her arm around Elise's shoulders again. "Now tell me about Seth."

"Why are you bringing him up?"

"Because I think he's all mixed up in this, too."

Pressing her lips together, Elise looked pointedly at Juliane. "You are too perceptive, but I'm only going to say this about him. He broke my heart. He made me realize I needed to come home. Because of him, I'm through with men forever."

"Well, I'm not glad that he broke your heart, but I'm glad you're home." Hugging Elise, Juliane meant every word. As she ended the hug, she eyed Elise. "Something tells me you're not going to stick with that last statement."

"Oh, yes, I am. Men are beasts—uncivilized monsters." Her head lowered, Elise picked at a loose thread on the quilt. "Okay, Jules, it's your turn. What's going on with Lukas?"

"Why are you pushing Lukas at me when you think men are uncivilized monsters?"

"Well, maybe not all men, but I've had enough heartache to last a lifetime. I don't want any more." Elise looked up. "So what gives with you two?"

Her heart thudding, Juliane wondered how she

was going to answer. She wasn't sure herself, so how could she explain anything to Elise? "I don't know— maybe nothing."

"What kind of an answer is that?"

Juliane shrugged. "About the only one I can give."

"But you do admit that you were a little jealous when we were singing together, right?"

"Okay, I was."

"I knew it!" Elise slapped her hands together. "So what are you going to do about it?"

Juliane frowned. "Nothing."

"Come on. You can't do nothing."

"Yes, I can."

"I'm not getting this. You're—"

"Elise, Lukas is a handsome man. I admit that I'm attracted to him, but there's a very good reason why I'm not going to act on that attraction. You proved your point, so let's not discuss it anymore."

"You can't throw out a statement like that and leave me hanging."

"Sure I can. I didn't press you for details about Seth, so let's call it even."

Her shoulders slumping, Elise sighed, then smiled. "Okay, you win."

"Good." Juliane hopped up from the bed. "You going to be all right now?"

"Yeah." Elise stood and gave Juliane another hug. "Thanks, Jules. You're the best."

"I don't know about being the best, but I'm tired. I'm headed to bed."

As Juliane turned to go, Elise reached out and touched her arm. "Wait. Before you go, I want to ask you about Dad."

Juliane turned back. "What about him?"

"I know you said he's not been drinking for months. Do you think he's stopped for good?"

"I don't know, Elise. I can only pray that's the case." Juliane couldn't help thinking about Lukas. He'd said the temptation never ends, but he was relying on God for his strength to overcome it. Had their dad given his drinking over to God and not told anyone? She couldn't be sure.

"I'll pray, too."

Juliane gave Elise another hug. "Thanks. Have a good night. I love you."

"I love you, too, Jules."

Descending the stairs, Juliane thought about all the emotional ups and downs of the day and realized she'd come out on the upside. Getting along with Elise was falling into place. Juliane could see that God would really work in her life if she got out of the way and let Him rule her life.

But getting out of the way wasn't always easy, especially where Lukas was concerned. She'd survived having him at the party, but each time they were together, she had more and more difficulty holding on to her vow not to let his good looks and kind actions draw her in and make her want more than friendship from him.

She knew God expected her to befriend Lukas, but surely God's plan didn't go beyond friendship, did it?

Lukas yanked his BlackBerry from the seat of his car as the ringing sounded over the noise coming from the radio. He had just left work, and someone was already calling him. Who? He glanced at the caller ID. Grandpa. Turning off the radio, Lukas tamped down his spike of fear as he answered the phone. He was usually the one to call, not Grandpa. If Grandpa was calling him, did that mean something was wrong—something so big that even his stubborn grandfather didn't believe he could handle it himself?

"Grandpa? What's wrong?"

"Are you on your way home?"

"I was getting ready to drive out of the parking lot at the plant."

"Good. Could you stop by my house before you go home?"

"I'll be there in five minutes."

With a sigh, Lukas ended the call. His grandfather sounded all right, but Lukas couldn't help but worry. He'd moved to Kellersburg to help. Should he be relieved or concerned when the older man asked for it?

Lukas pulled into the driveway at his grandfather's house. As he got out of the car, big white snowflakes started falling. Unlike the storm a couple of weeks ago, these flakes fell in a lazy pattern against the darkened sky.

After taking the front steps in one bound, he let himself into the house. A delicious smell coming from the kitchen greeted him. "Grandpa, I'm here. What do you need?"

His grandfather came out of the kitchen, a pot holder in one hand. "Oh, good. You got here very quickly."

"I know. I was worried." Clearly, there was no reason to worry. His grandfather seemed fine. So why had he called? "Tell me what you need. I can't stay long because we're having the dress rehearsal for the Winter Festival tonight."

"You need to slow down and enjoy life a little. You are pushing yourself too hard."

Before Lukas could make an argument against the statement, the doorbell rang. His grandfather rushed to the front door. "My company is here."

"Grandpa, I don't have time to visit. Who—" The word stuck in Lukas's mouth as Juliane and Dot walked into the house.

"Ladies, thank you so much for coming." Ferd closed the door and ushered Dot and Juliane farther into the living room.

"Thank you for inviting us." Juliane took off her

coat and helped Dot out of her coat, then handed them to Ferd.

Ferd trotted off to put the coats in the bedroom while Lukas stood there wondering what was going on. "So Grandpa invited you over?"

Juliane nodded. "We're here for supper. Didn't he tell you?"

His heart tripping, Lukas fought back a smile. So Grandpa was matchmaking again. This time Lukas didn't even mind. "No, he didn't. Just told me that he needed my help."

"Help eating the food maybe." Dot chuckled and held up a bag. "I brought cookies. I hope you like them."

"I'm sure I will." Lukas wasn't sure whether he wanted to wring his grandfather's neck or hug it.

Ferd returned to the living room. "Ladies, please have a seat."

"Can't we do something to help?" Juliane asked.

Ferd shook his head. "You relax. Lukas will help me in the kitchen."

Lukas strode after his grandfather, then glared at him as he removed a large baking dish from the oven. "Why did you ask me over and not tell me this was an invitation for supper?"

Ferd set the dish on top of the stove. "I thought you might say you did not have time, but I knew if I said I needed your help, you would come. You are such a good grandson, and I know I can count on your help."

If Lukas didn't know better, he'd believe his grandfather was engaging in flattery. But Lukas had to acknowledge that his grandfather's response was genuine. "Okay, thanks for inviting me. How can I help?"

"You can put the red cabbage in a bowl, find a serving spoon for it and put it on the table."

Eyeing the casserole dish on the stove, Lukas did as his grandfather instructed. "Is that your baked spaetzle with ham and cheese?"

"Yes, I promised Dot and Juliane last week at the senior center that I would cook them some good German food."

"This is great, Grandpa. You haven't cooked in a long time." The delicious aromas wafting through the kitchen made Lukas regret that he'd ever been ashamed of his German heritage. "You aren't wearing yourself out with all this work, are you?"

Ferd waved the pot holder at Lukas. "No need to worry yourself. I am very fit now that the doctors have fixed me up. I am feeling wonderful."

"Well, don't start doing too much."

"I am fine. That doctor said so." Nodding, Ferd placed napkins at each place setting. "I am glad I did as you said and listened to the doctors."

"That's good to know."

Wagging a finger at Lukas, Ferd placed a trivet on the table and the casserole on top of it. "I listened to you, so I want you to listen to me. I have asked Dot to go to the Valentine's banquet at church, and she said yes."

"That's nice. When did you do that?"

"During the homecoming party for Juliane's sister." Ferd looked up at Lukas and stabbed a finger into his chest. "Listen. I'm not finished talking yet. You ask Juliane to go."

"I'll think about it." Lukas didn't want to argue with his grandfather, especially with Juliane in the next room.

"No, just thinking about it is not enough. You must do it."

"Grandpa, save this for another time. You have guests."

Ferd frowned. "All right, but I will expect you to ask her."

Lukas hurried into the living room to get away from his grandfather and his insistence about asking Juliane to the Valentine's banquet. "Okay, ladies, supper is served."

After everyone was seated, Lukas gave thanks for the food. As they started to eat, he said a silent prayer that his grandfather wouldn't embarrass him by mentioning the banquet. Lukas was thrilled that Dot and his grandfather were enjoying each other's company, but why did he have to demand that Lukas have a date, too? Especially Juliane, who had shown so little interest in his company?

"Are you and Lukas ready for the Valentine's banquet?" Ferd took Juliane's plate and served her some of the casserole.

"Yes. Everything is set. My cousin Nathan finally agreed to be the master of ceremonies."

Holding his breath, Lukas prayed that his grandfather wouldn't continue to talk about the banquet. Lukas decided to change the subject. "We have to get through the Winter Festival first. This new snowfall will be great for the festival."

"And the forecast calls for more snow on Friday night. I hope it's not another blizzard." Juliane took a bite of her food. "Ferd, this is delicious. What is it called?"

"Baked spaetzle with ham and cheese. It is a dish that my mother made when I was a boy in Germany."

"I had no idea you were such a wonderful chef."

"Thank you."

Lukas didn't miss the fact that Juliane's compliment made his grandfather blush. But then, she'd endeared herself to him from the beginning. Lukas was beginning to feel the same way. He'd been smitten with her even when she'd been trying to ignore him because she thought he was still a drunk.

Could he get up enough nerve to ask her to the banquet? Even if he did, would she say yes? Why was he torturing himself with these questions?

Following his grandfather's example and fulfilling

his request was something Lukas knew he should do. He wanted to ask Juliane for a date, but he'd satisfied himself with seeing her at church and choir practice and things like Elise's party.

Now was the time for him to step up and quit being a coward. Taking a big bite of the spaetzle, he told himself that he would ask Juliane to the banquet, not just to please his grandfather but also to please himself. He had the courage. Tonight he would accept his grandfather's challenge. Then it would be up to Juliane.

Throughout the rest of the meal while the others talked, Lukas tried to figure out how he would ask her. He went over a dozen different scenarios in his mind. He rehearsed and rehashed them until he nearly talked himself out of going through with it. Every plan seemed inadequate.

"Dot and I will do the cleanup, then we are going to watch a video that I rented." Ferd's comment shook Lukas from his troubled thoughts. "You young folks can run along to your practice."

Lukas looked up from his plate and found Juliane staring at him. His heart beat in double time as he smiled at her. "Are you ready to go? I can drive. No sense in taking two cars since you have to come back here to take Dot home."

"Excellent plan." Ferd stood and stacked the plates. "We will see you later."

Lukas could tell by his grandfather's look that he

was reminding Lukas of their earlier discussion. Hoping to get out of the kitchen before Grandpa said anything about it, Lukas hurried Juliane into the living room and got their coats.

When Lukas returned, he helped Juliane with her coat, then shrugged into his own. Seeing Grandpa and Dot step into the living room, Lukas opened the front door. He waved, and Juliane called goodbye as he rushed her outside.

As Lukas backed out of the driveway, Juliane glanced over at him. "Are you afraid we're going to be late or something? You barely gave me a chance to say thanks."

Lukas pointed at the clock on the dash. "We don't have much time. Besides, I thought we should get an early start. I might have to drive slower since the streets will probably be slick from the snow."

"I suppose you're right."

"Anyway, you can tell him thanks when we come back."

Nodding, Juliane looked straight ahead as if she were lost in thought. He should ask her now, but he didn't know how to bring it up. Maybe he should just blurt it out. Get it over with. Otherwise, he'd be thinking about it all night rather than concentrating on the choir program. He might even lose his nerve it he waited.

He took a deep breath. "Juliane, would you go to the Valentine's banquet with me?"

Chapter Twelve

That familiar jittery feeling filled Juliane's chest. This invitation was the last thing she had expected to hear from him tonight. Hoping he wouldn't see the indecision in her eyes, she concentrated on the snowflakes instead of looking at him.

Her pulse pounded in time to the wipers that pushed away the snow that stuck to the windshield. She wanted to say yes, but her tongue felt frozen.

Glancing over at her, he slowed the car as the traffic light turned red. A half laugh, half sigh came out of his mouth. "Guess I should've known you wouldn't go with me."

"No. No, I do want to go with you." Juliane put a hand on Lukas's arm.

"Are you sure? You certainly took long enough to reply."

"I think I was in shock." Had she just admitted

that? Her brain was definitely on overload. She took a deep breath to calm herself. "I'd be honored to be your date."

A slow smile curved his lips as the light changed and he cautiously went through the intersection. "Great. We can make some definite plans. Did you know that Grandpa is taking Dot?"

Juliane nodded. "I think they're such a cute couple. How do you feel about it?"

"Whatever makes Grandpa happy makes me happy. At least most of the time."

"Are we going to double-date?" Juliane wondered whether having the older couple with them would be the perfect thing on this first date.

"That's possible. I'll check with Grandpa."

"It's up to you." Juliane thought she detected a little disappointment in Lukas's response, or was she imagining that he wasn't thrilled about having his grandfather and his date along?

"Do your parents usually go to this?"

"It all depends." Juliane couldn't help thinking about the year that her father got drunk and her mother had to go alone because she'd volunteered to be part of the program. Juliane later heard her mother crying. The sound had broken Juliane's heart and made her wary of ever giving her heart away. But something about Lukas made her question that resolve. Was he truly the man she could trust with her heart?

"I was thinking if they're going, we should have your dad sing one number. He sings great. What do you think?"

Juliane shook her head. "We've already got the whole thing planned, and I don't want to change it now."

"That wouldn't take much. Put him in place of one of my songs."

"I don't think that's a good idea. You never know when he'll have store business that interferes," Juliane said, fearing that not only store business could be a problem, but his sudden falling off the wagon. She couldn't take the chance.

"Well, if you change your mind, I'll be glad to relinquish one of my songs."

"Why are you so eager to get my dad involved in this?"

"I just think he's got a gift."

Yeah, a gift for making his family miserable from time to time with his drinking. Juliane wanted so badly to tell Lukas about her father's problem. Lukas would certainly understand, but she couldn't bring herself to divulge the family secret. She'd kept it for so long, she wasn't sure she could ever talk about it with anyone, even Lukas. Her father's problem remained an embarrassment that she couldn't share. Instead of dwelling on that, she focused on her happiness at being Lukas's date.

When Lukas stopped the car in the church parking lot, Juliane forced herself not to jump out of the car and run into the church. She wanted to find Elise and let her know that Lukas had asked her to the banquet.

Juliane walked beside Lukas as they made their way toward the side door of the church. "The snow's beautiful, isn't it?"

"Not so much when I have to shovel it."

Juliane laughed and turned her face up to the sky and let the snowflakes kiss her cheeks. "I suppose after that incident at my house, you aren't too fond of the snow, but it is beautiful. It makes everything seem so clean and pure."

"Like a couple of verses in the Bible that talk about being whiter than snow."

"Yeah."

"My friend Bill used to remind me of those verses when I had trouble believing that God would forgive me for all the rotten things I've done." Lukas opened the door, and they went inside.

"We're all sinners, saved by grace."

"Thanks for reminding me of that, too."

After hanging their coats on the rack in the hallway, they entered the sanctuary. Juliane looked around, hoping to see Elise, but only Pastor Tom and a couple of other choir members were there. Lukas immediately started talking with Pastor Tom, and Juliane headed to the restroom since they'd arrived early. The snowy streets hadn't slowed them down after all.

In the restroom, Juliane brushed her hair as she checked her reflection in the mirror. Her cheeks were flushed. Was it from the cold or the excitement of having Lukas ask her for a date? She had to get a grip. She was acting like a schoolgirl who'd been asked out for the first time and could hardly wait to tell her friends. Chuckling, she had to admit that was the way she felt—like she was sixteen again.

As Juliane went back down the hall toward the sanctuary, Elise was coming in through the side door from the parking lot. Juliane rushed forward and grabbed one of Elise's arms and pulled her to one side. "I've got to tell you something."

Elise drew back and looked at her with concern. "What?"

Leaning close to Elise, Juliane cupped her hand near Elise's ear. "Tonight on the way to church, Lukas asked me to the Valentine's banquet."

Elise stepped back, raised her hands and gave a silence scream. "I'm assuming you said yes."

Grinning from ear to ear, Juliane nodded. "I could hardly wait to tell you."

Elise hugged Juliane. "I'm so thrilled for you."

"Now we have to get you a date."

"Oh, no. That's why I volunteered to work in the kitchen."

"Come on, Elise. We could all go together."

Elise put her hands on her hips. "Now think about it. Where would I find a date?"

"Okay, you've got me there. There aren't too many eligible men in this town that we aren't related to in some way. Or they're too old or too young."

"That's one of the big pluses of moving back here. It's the perfect place to live and have no temptation to get involved with a man."

"You're going to eat those words one of these days."

"Just like you?" Elise raised her eyebrows. "For someone who only days ago didn't intend to do anything about your interest in Lukas, you're certainly excited."

"I know, I can't believe it either."

"We'd better get to practice."

Juliane followed Elise into the sanctuary and hoped the event would be able to live up to her excitement.

Friday morning Juliane rolled out of bed, threw on her robe and wandered into the kitchen. After she put some water on to boil for tea, she went out to the front porch to retrieve the newspaper. Gazing at the newly fallen snow glittering in the sunshine, she knew it was a perfect day for the start of the Winter Festival. The first events would begin late this afternoon and go through Sunday night. The choir was scheduled to make their first performance at six o'clock in front of the courthouse in the town square.

As Juliane went back inside, she met Elise, who was coming down the stairs. "Good morning, Jules. Looks like a great day."

"It is." Juliane's words came out in a harsh whisper.

"Juliane, what's wrong with your voice?"

"I don't know." The raspy sound made her stomach sink. How was she going to sing in the festival when her voice sounded like a croaking frog?

"Do you feel okay?"

"Yeah. What am I going to do?" She touched her throat as the whispery words sounded in her ears. "I can't sing with a voice like this."

"Is your throat sore?"

Shaking her head, Juliane felt like crying. She didn't want to talk for fear her voice would get worse. Why was this happening? There had been no signs of this the evening before when Lukas and she had gone over their solos and duet one more time.

"Maybe your voice is hoarse from the dry air in the house." Elise headed for the kitchen. "Let's have some tea. That might help."

Juliane walked into the kitchen, her big fuzzy slippers shuffling against the hardwood floor. She sat at the kitchen table while she sipped the cinnamon tea and ate the cream of wheat that Elise served her. The warm liquid and hot cereal went down easily, but when she tried to speak, nothing changed. Her voice still croaked.

"I'll call Dad and tell him you won't be in this morning."

Juliane nodded in agreement and continued to drink the tea.

After Elise finished talking on the kitchen phone, she turned. "Dad wants me to come in for a little while to help this morning since you can't come in. Will you be okay?"

"Yeah," Juliane whispered.

"I'm going to call Lukas, too, and tell him what's happening. Do you have his number?"

Feeling hopeless, Juliane nodded again and squeaked, "On my BlackBerry."

Juliane listened to the one-sided conversation but couldn't figure out what contingency plans they were discussing.

Covering the receiver with a hand, Elise turned. "Do you have the CD of the numbers you're doing?"

Juliane nodded.

Elise took her hand away from the mouthpiece. "I can practice with Juliane's CD. You can come over to the house during your lunch hour, and we can run through it then. Hopefully, that'll be good enough to get us through this evening's performance."

"What's happening?" Juliane managed to whisper, then finished her cereal and drank the last of her tea.

"I guess I'm going to sing your part. I've listened to it enough times that I think I should be able to do it without much trouble."

"I suppose." Juliane couldn't believe after all of the time she'd spent practicing that Elise was going to waltz in and take her part. It wasn't Elise's fault that this had happened, but somehow it didn't seem fair. Juliane fought against the jealousy that pricked her heart.

"Maybe you should go back to bed and rest now that you've eaten. What do you think?"

"I guess." Juliane shrugged. What would be the point in that? Her only problem was not having a voice. Otherwise, she didn't feel bad at all, but then she'd never had laryngitis before, so what did she know? Besides, Elise and Lukas had already decided that they were doing the singing today, so why did it matter whether she got better or not?

Elise cleared the dishes and put them in the dishwasher. "I'll get dressed and spend a couple hours at the store helping Dad before I come back home to practice with Lukas. Dad's expecting to be extra busy because of the festival."

"Okay." Juliane felt about as energetic as a rag doll. Maybe she wasn't feeling so good, after all.

Elise stopped on her way out the door and pointed at Juliane. "You. Off to bed."

Smiling halfheartedly, Juliane got up and did as her sister instructed—probably for the first time in her life. She climbed back into bed, not even bothering to take off her robe.

A couple of hours later, Juliane awakened. Sunlight shone through the curtains on her window and brightened the room. She glanced at the clock radio. The bright red digital numbers read ten o'clock. She sat up in a panic. What was she still doing in bed?

Putting a hand to her head, she remembered. Her voice. She tried to speak. Not only did her voice come out in the hideous raspy tones, but her throat hurt when she swallowed and she felt hot. She should call the doctor. She was thankful for living in a small town where getting in to see her doctor was still relatively easy even without an appointment.

After making a quick trip to the doctor and the pharmacy for the antibiotic that he prescribed, Juliane drove back home feeling more miserable than ever. Strep throat. She hadn't had strep throat since she was a kid. There went the whole Winter Festival down the drain, at least for her.

When she got back home, she took the medicine and went back to bed. She was feeling worse by the minute. Chills and fever made her cold one minute and hot the next. Awful couldn't even describe how she felt.

A half hour later, Elise came rushing into Juliane's bedroom. "How do you feel?"

Raising her head off the pillow, Juliane waved Elise out of the room. "Don't come in. Strep throat."

"Oh, no. Wouldn't want to get that." Elise backed up to the door. "You went to the doctor?"

Juliane nodded. "Just got back."

"You should've called me. I could've taken you."

"No. You don't want this." Closing her eyes, Juliane swallowed even though it hurt. "Go."

"Yeah, I wasn't thinking. Do you need anything?"

Motioning for Elise to leave, Juliane shook her head.

"Well, Lukas can't get away from work, so we're going to try to run through this together at church about a half an hour before the performance. Pastor Tom said he'd go through the music with me late this afternoon." Elise sighed. "I'm going back to the store because Dad still needs help. Mom said to call her if you need anything. I'm just going to grab a bite to eat before I go."

Listening to Elise's agenda made Juliane tired. Closing her eyes, she snuggled under the covers and drifted off to sleep.

Laughter accompanied the slamming of a door. Voices sounded in the hall. Slowly opening her eyes, Juliane rolled over and glanced at the clock, the only light in the darkened room. This time it read seven-thirty. Had she slept that long? She swallowed. Her throat still killed. Her head pounded. When was she going to start getting better?

A knock sounded on the door. A second later Elise poked her head into the room. "Hi, feeling any better?"

Juliane frowned and shook her head.

"Someone's here to see you."

When Lukas appeared from behind Elise in the hallway, Juliane wanted to die. Running a hand through her hair, she knew she must look terrible. Why did he have to see her this way?

"Do you feel like eating? I brought you some soup."

As miserable as she felt, Lukas's kindness touched her. She managed to croak, "Don't come in."

"Well, I have to get the soup to you somehow." Lukas chuckled. "I'll be back."

Juliane lay in the bed and wished she had the energy to at least comb her hair, but she didn't. In a few minutes, Lukas and Elise returned, each wearing face masks that Juliane recognized as being left over from the house renovations. Elise carried a tray while Lukas carried a large steaming bowl and a large glass of orange juice.

Despite her sore throat, she laughed and rose to a sitting position. "Are you here to rob me or feed me?"

"Your voice sounds better." Elise's words came through in muffled tones. "We're here to feed you homemade chicken soup that Lukas bought from one of the booths at the festival."

"That sounds good, but how did you find those masks?"

Elise set the tray down over Juliane's legs. "I was looking for something in the pantry a week or so ago, and I saw them. I had no idea we'd have any use for them."

"Here's your soup." Lukas set the bowl and a spoon on the tray, as well as a few crackers and the juice. "Just what the doctor ordered."

Juliane looked up at him as a warm fluttery feeling filled her chest. She was sure he was smiling behind that mask if the twinkle in his blue eyes was any indication. She wasn't sure whether her light-headed feeling came from being sick or having Lukas so near.

"Thanks." Feeling a little self-conscious about having an audience while she ate, especially a masked one, Juliane laughed. "You guys are cracking me up with those masks. I'm beginning to feel like Typhoid Mary." She picked up the spoon. "How did the performance go?"

Lukas patted Elise on the back. "Your sister is amazing. She did a fantastic job. Everything was perfect."

Elise smiled at Lukas. "He exaggerates."

"No, I don't. Your professional experience was an asset. And we're all set for tomorrow's performance."

"That's a relief. We won't be running around like crazy again tomorrow." Elise headed for the door. "I'm going to call Mom and Dad and tell them how you're doing. They wanted to come over, but I told them they shouldn't. We don't want them to get sick."

"Better safe than sorry," Lukas said as Elise left the room.

Taking a spoonful of soup, Juliane tried not to let Lukas's praise of Elise bother her. Why was she twisting herself in knots over nothing? A few weeks ago she didn't want anything to do with Lukas. Now she was worried that he might take an interest in her sister. Juliane knew she should get her head on straight. As she sipped the warm liquid, it soothed her throat, as well as soothing her thoughts.

Lukas leaned against the doorjamb, his mask still in place and the twinkle still in his eyes. "How's the soup?"

She gave the thumbs-up sign.

"Oh, I forgot you shouldn't be talking. I'll go and let you finish eating. Take care of yourself. Get some more rest. I want you healthy for the Valentine's banquet." He blew her a kiss.

Blowing him a return kiss, she smiled, and her heart raced.

How would she react to a real kiss? Would that old incident haunt her, or was that completely a part of the past and no problem now? Why had that thought even entered her mind? Must be foggy thinking brought on by her fever.

After Juliane finished eating, she set the tray aside and lay back in the bed. Worn-out from eating, she didn't have enough energy to keep her eyes open. She snuggled under the covers again. Even though she was tired, she couldn't seem to go to sleep.

Hearing Lukas heap praise on Elise created fertile ground for the seeds of jealousy to sprout. She couldn't let them grow. Lukas had asked her to the banquet, not Elise. And Elise had been so happy for her. So there was no reason to be jealous. Juliane rolled over in her bed and pounded her pillow. Why did that ugly green monster spring up at the slightest provocation?

While Juliane lay in her bed listening to the two of them laugh together in the other room, she tried to drive that into her head. She didn't want to be jealous. She and Elise had started getting along so well. Juliane couldn't let this incident sabotage all the good feelings that had developed between them.

Lukas had braved coming over to see her and taken the chance of being exposed to her illness. He'd brought her soup. Why should she doubt that he cared?

Chapter Thirteen

Nervous anticipation had plagued Lukas all day while he'd waited to attend the Valentine's banquet. Thankfully, in the two weeks since the Winter Festival, Juliane had fully recovered from her strep throat. Fighting the tension that buzzed through his body, he opened the door for her. "Be careful. The parking lot is like a skating rink. I'm glad we dropped Grandpa and Dot off at the door. I suppose you should've gotten out, too."

"But I wanted to be with you." Juliane smiled up at him and slipped her arm through his. "I'll hang on to you. So as long as you don't fall down, I won't either."

Her statement warmed his heart but still didn't take away the anxious feeling that wouldn't let go. How many times had he used alcohol to fortify himself in social situations like this? He prayed that those days were gone forever.

What did he have to be nervous about? Juliane was his friend. But he couldn't forget that he wanted more than friendship.

As they slipped their way across the parking lot, not only her touch, but also the way she put her trust in him made his heart race. He shouldn't be nervous, but he was. He'd spent weeks practicing with her in the choir, going to the coffee shop or grabbing a quick bite to eat with her. But tonight was different. This was a real date, even with his grandfather and Dot along.

As Lukas helped Juliane take off her coat, he couldn't help admiring the way she looked in her sleek red dress. He hadn't seen it before because she'd been wearing her coat when he'd picked her up for their date. He wanted to compliment her, but his thought processes froze like the icicles hanging from the church eaves.

Before Lukas could come up with the right thing to say, Dot reached over and touched the silky-looking fabric. "Juliane, that's a lovely dress. Did you get it from your store?"

"Thanks. I did." Juliane nodded and smiled. "It was a special order I made before Christmas, but it was back-ordered, so it came in too late. I'm so glad I have a chance to wear it now."

"It is perfect for Valentine's." Dot slipped her arm through Ferd's.

Ferd turned to smile at Dot. "You look lovely, too, in your bright red sweater. It matches my red tie."

"It does. Thank you. It's good for a cold night."

Lukas hoped for another opportunity to tell Juliane how lovely she looked. If he said something now, he figured it would seem lame. He was out of practice giving compliments to women. He'd rarely taken a woman out since he'd been sober. When he'd been drinking he was never nervous on dates. He'd been the life of the party, but he'd been getting his bravado from alcohol. Not anymore.

Over the past few weeks, he'd realized that Juliane meant a lot to him. Tonight's date was more important than any of the others. He wished for a perfect evening. He didn't want to mess up, because she was taking a chance on him—a guy she knew to have a big flaw. Still, she'd agreed to go out with him.

While they made their way toward the fellowship hall, laughter and conversation filtered into the hallway. Swallowing the lump in his throat, he escorted Juliane into the room. The aroma of garlic and tomato sauce wafted through the air. The red-and-white-checked tablecloths on the round tables throughout the hall signaled the evening's Italian theme. Centered on each table, red candles flickered inside hurricane glasses filled with red and white hearts, while posters of famous Italian landmarks decorated the walls.

Leading the way to their table, Lukas resisted the urge to run a finger around the inside of his shirt collar. His necktie felt as though it was choking him.

Soon after they were seated, Juliane's parents and Val and Eric joined them at the table for eight. Lively talk swirled around Lukas as he tried to think of something to say. What was the matter with him tonight? She was going to think he was a very boring date.

A few minutes later, Nathan stepped to the microphone and quieted the crowd. He gave thanks for the food. While soft instrumental music played over the sound system, the teens from the church youth group served the Caesar salads. Soon everyone around Lukas was eating, and the need for conversation waned. He began to relax.

Val patted Juliane's arm. "I'm sorry you had to miss the Winter Festival, but I'm glad you recovered in time for this."

"Me, too." Juliane turned to Lukas. "I'm just glad I didn't give it to Lukas or Elise. They were both so good to me while I was sick."

"Everyone here is glad that you didn't share your strep throat. Otherwise, you would've been scrambling to come up with some new entertainment." Lukas glanced around the table.

Even as the words came out of his mouth, he knew he'd blown it again. Here he was talking about everyone, when he should be saying how happy he was to have her here. Could he rewind the clock and start the evening over? Too bad that wasn't possible.

While Lukas sat there stewing, the salad plates were whisked away and replaced with the entrée, chicken parmesan, and baskets full of garlic bread. Maybe he should eat rather than talk. He'd let the others discuss the success of the Winter Festival, local news and the weather.

As folks finished their dessert, Nathan went to the microphone. "Ladies and gentlemen, we are proud to have some wonderful entertainment for you tonight. First, we have, straight from her world tour aboard world-renowned cruise ships, Elise Keller."

Elise trotted out from the kitchen wearing a sparkly black dress. Loud applause greeted her as she took the microphone from Nathan. "Thank you, everyone. I believe our master of ceremonies is exaggerating my credentials a little."

The crowd laughed, and Elise grinned as Nathan cued the accompaniment. "I hope you'll enjoy the love songs I've chosen to sing."

As the intro faded, Elise's voice filled the hall. The words of the song "Valentine" settled into Lukas's brain. He wished somehow he could convey that message to Juliane. He glanced her way, but she wasn't paying any attention to him. Her eyes were focused on her sister.

When Elise finished singing, loud clapping and

whistles filled the air. She bowed and smiled. As Elise began to sing, "When You Say Nothing at All," Lukas caught Juliane's eye. His heart hummed along with the soft guitar chords. Could he speak right to Juliane's heart without saying anything? So far tonight he hoped that was the case, because he wasn't doing a very good job with the spoken word.

Elise sang a few more songs, and when the last notes of her final song sounded, again the crowd erupted in applause. Smiling, Elise took several bows before handing the microphone back to Nathan.

"Let's give Elise another round of applause before we welcome out next performer." Clapping filled the room, then Nathan introduced Jasper Cornett, who soon had the crowd doubled over with laughter as he told jokes and did his impressions.

Jasper finished, and again Nathan took charge. "Next Lukas Frey will entertain us."

Making his way to the stage, Lukas tried to calm his nerves as applause sounded around him. He hadn't been nearly this nervous singing before the whole town at the Winter Festival, but this was different. Juliane was here, and he wanted to impress her.

As Lukas reached the stage, he took the microphone. "Thank you. This first song was made famous by Nat King Cole. Although I can't duplicate his rendition, I hope you'll enjoy my version of 'Unforgettable.'"

Lukas wanted to sing the song just for Juliane, but

he was almost afraid to look in her direction. He let his gaze roam through the room and finally rest on her. His heart beat in double time when she smiled at him. He was a goner, and she was definitely unforgettable. When he finished he took a few seconds to acknowledge the applause, but quickly launched into his second song, "Till There Was You." He hoped Juliane realized both songs were for her, along with all the rest of the songs in his set.

As Lukas finished, again applause thundered. Nathan walked back to the stage while Lukas rushed into the hallway where he met Elise. "You have the costumes?"

Nodding, Elise held out a plastic bag. "The stuff's in here."

After Lukas donned the shaggy brown wig and mustache, he glanced up at Elise, who wore a wig with long, straight black hair. "Do you think we'll pass for Sonny and Cher?"

"Let's find out." Elise signaled to Nathan from the hallway.

"Folks, I know you enjoyed the entertainment so far. Now we have another treat for you." Nathan waved them onto the stage.

Lukas and Elise ran out as the first notes of "I Got You Babe" rang through the air along with the laughter and clapping from the crowd. After Lukas and Elise finished, they removed their wigs and immediately launched into another duet, "Love Will Keep Us Alive."

When the last notes of the song sounded, Lukas and Elise received a standing ovation. As he surveyed the crowd, Juliane was standing and clapping. Hers was the only ovation Lukas needed.

He returned to his seat amid loud cheering. In addition to Juliane's approval, Lukas basked in the pride that registered on his grandfather's face. Lukas knew he'd come a long way since those days when his grandfather had given up on him, but he reminded himself that he still had to take one day at a time.

The evening's entertainment concluded with the not-so-newlywed game. Val and Eric were the first couple called while cheers and jeers emanated from the surrounding tables. Then Juliane's aunt Eileen and uncle Carl, her parents and Tim and Melanie Drake made their way to the stage.

Lukas leaned over to Juliane. "This ought to be interesting. I'm waiting to see whether my assistant manager and his wife can beat your parents."

"We'll see. They might have a good chance. I don't think my parents will be very good at this game. My dad can't remember what my mom said yesterday." Juliane laughed. "How's he going to remember her favorite color or whatever questions Nathan decided to use?"

"We'll see." Settling back in his chair, Lukas

listened to the questions, the answers and the laughter that ensued and wondered whether he could make a good husband. He'd just about given up on that idea until he'd gotten to know Juliane.

Joy captured Juliane's heart as she sat in Lukas's car. The banquet had been everything she'd imagined. She couldn't remember when she'd had a better time. Lukas gripped the steering wheel, his attention on Ferd, who climbed the steps and unlocked his door. Turning, he waved before going inside.

"I wish he didn't want so much independence. I always worry that he'll fall, but he insists he doesn't need any help." Sighing, Lukas put the car in gear and pulled into the street.

"He and Dot were so cute tonight."

"I think he kissed her good-night when he walked her to the door." Lukas chuckled. "I couldn't tell for sure in the dark."

"Keeping tabs on your grandfather?"

"Someone has to."

While they rode in silence, Juliane wondered who was going to keep tabs on her heart. Lukas was winning it over day by day and little by little. She still wasn't sure that was wise. But one thing she knew for sure—she hoped Lukas followed his grandfather's example when saying good-night.

She was ready for Lukas's kiss.

Not a drunken kiss, but a kiss that he gave her because he knew her and knew where he was. A kiss given with tenderness and caring. She'd been thinking about it ever since he'd asked her to the banquet. She wanted to experience his kiss, but thinking about it was tying her insides into knots. She should put her mind on something else.

"When did you and Elise cook up that bit with the Sonny and Cher costumes? That wasn't in the original plan."

"During those last-minute practices for the Winter Festival. Elise had done a number like that during a cruise show and thought it would be fun."

"Everyone loved it. You guys did great tonight. I wish I could've heard you at the Winter Festival, too."

"I wish I could've sung with you." He pulled into her driveway and shut off his car.

"We'll have another chance."

"I hope so." He reached into the backseat and brought out a small bag decorated with red hearts. "I got you a little gift. Happy Valentine's Day."

Juliane's heart fluttered. "But I didn't get you anything."

"I didn't expect anything. Your going to the banquet with me was a gift." The intensity in his gaze took her breath away.

She took the bag and opened it. A little wooden house sat nestled in the tissue paper. She lifted it out.

"It's a German weather house." Lukas pointed to the figurines standing in the doorways on either side of the thermometer mounted on the front. "When the weather is bad the man comes out slightly, and when the weather is sunny the woman comes out."

"It's adorable. I love it." Looking up, she saw relief in his eyes. "Thank you."

"I have to give Grandpa credit. He suggested it." Lukas pointed to the thermometer. "The temperature indicates that I should get you out of this cold car."

"Good idea." Juliane laughed and put the weather house back in the bag and slipped her arm through the handles.

Walking to her front porch in the cold night air, she snuggled against him as he draped an arm around her shoulders.

They skirted an icy patch in front of the steps. "You should get some deicer for that spot. I wouldn't want you to fall and break something."

"You're right." She was falling all right—falling for this wonderful man. She hoped it wouldn't mean a broken heart. When they stepped onto the porch, she turned to face him. Her heart hammered as he smiled. "I had a great time tonight."

"Me, too." He stepped closer.

Her pulse raced with anticipation as she raised her head to look into his eyes. She couldn't miss the caring in them. Every nerve hummed. He gently pulled her into his arms.

He lowered his mouth to hers. But at the last second, as she was about to close her eyes, that old incident raced through her mind in a blinding flash, leaving her shaken. Alarm took over, and she turned away.

A huge lump formed in her throat. All evening she'd waited for this moment, anticipated this kiss. Why had she panicked? She wished the porch would open up and swallow her.

He stepped back, a troubled expression clouding his features as his eyebrows knit in a frown. He didn't say anything, just stared at her.

Embarrassed, she quickly turned to the door and fumbled to fit her key in the lock, the gift bag dangling from her arm. "Thanks again. I had a lovely time."

"Did I do something wrong?"

She hunched her shoulders, afraid to turn and face him. Misery marched in and swept away all the good feelings of the evening. She thought she'd forgiven him, thought she'd put the past behind them. Why had she let that bad memory ruin everything? How was she going to explain?

Taking a deep breath, she shook her head. "I'm sorry, it's not your fault. It's mine."

"Would you care to explain, or should I go?"

She couldn't let him go. He deserved an explanation. Maybe getting that event out in the open would put the relationship on a better footing. Isn't that what she wanted?

She turned, anguish pressing down on her chest. "Don't go. I want to explain. Please come in."

"Are you sure?"

Not trusting her voice, she nodded and opened the door. She headed for the couch and sat on one end. She looked up at Lukas, who stood hesitantly just inside the door. "Please sit wherever you want."

"Okay." He took the chair he'd sat in on his very first visit.

Swallowing hard, she looked at him. What must he think? Just as Juliane started to say something, Elise came bopping into the room.

"Hi, you guys."

"Hi," Juliane and Lukas chorused.

Elise smiled. "Okay, I can see I'm intruding. I'm off to bed. Wouldn't want to disturb a couple of lovebirds."

If Elise only knew what she was disturbing. As Elise scurried upstairs, Juliane scooted forward on the couch, sitting on the very edge. She closed her eyes for a moment and gathered her courage with a little prayer. *Lord, help me.*

"Are you okay?"

Opening her eyes, she nodded. "I hope you understand."

"What happened out there?"

She nodded again. There was no easy way to talk

about this, so she might as well lay it all out there—
the story and her unexpected reaction. No sugarcoat-
ing, just the truth. "Will you promise not to stop me
until I'm done?"

"Okay." His voice resonated with uncertainty.

Unable to look at him, she stared at her hands as
she twisted them in her lap. Taking a deep breath, she
launched into the story. In a monotone, she went
through the events of that night, explaining how
terribly scared she'd been. When she finished, silence
captured the room. Finally, she forced herself to look
at Lukas. Hurt and sorrow emanated from his eyes
before he averted his gaze and hung his head.

"I'm so sorry I hurt you." He shook his head. "I
don't remember any of that."

"I know."

"But when you handed me my keys the night you
helped with Grandpa, I felt some connection with
you, me and a set of keys. I dismissed it, but now I
know why I had that thought." He stood. "Please
forgive me. I'll leave now."

"No. I've already forgiven you." Juliane jumped to
her feet. "I'm the one who's sorry. I panicked for absolutely no reason. You aren't that man anymore,
and I know that now, but somehow some deep dark
part of my mind didn't get the message. Forgive me
for ruining our evening."

"You're asking for my forgiveness?"

"Yes." She stepped closer. "Can we try that kiss again?"

A little smile tugged at the corners of his mouth— a very kissable mouth. "You're sure?"

"Very." Standing on her tiptoes and lacing her fingers at the back of his neck, she went gladly into his arms and lifted her face to his. He brushed his lips against hers. She closed her eyes and old worries faded as he deepened the kiss. Contentment replaced her old concerns. Her heart opened to the future as the past fled.

Chapter Fourteen

Popping out of bed, Juliane looked at Lukas's weather house sitting on the nightstand. The little man had inched his way out. More bad weather? Hadn't they had enough of that this winter? Despite the little house's unwelcome prediction, its presence reminded Juliane of the man behind the gift and the love that was developing between them. Finally getting the incident with Lukas out in the open gave her a new peace.

A month had passed since the night of the banquet, and they'd spent every weekend together often doing something with Tim and Melanie Drake. At least once a week, they ate dinner with Ferd and Dot. This time together created a sense of contentment until she thought about how she hadn't completely faced the issues surrounding the possibility that Lukas could relapse on his sobriety.

Throwing on her robe and slippers, she pushed away that troublesome thought. She only wanted to think about the fun evening she'd spent with Lukas and the Drakes, playing board games well past midnight.

As Juliane made her way to get the newspaper on the front porch, she noted that a silent house meant that Elise was still sleeping. Opening the front door, Juliane gasped. Bad weather for sure. At least a six-inch blanket of snow covered everything in sight. When she closed the door and turned toward the kitchen, she spied Elise coming down the stairs.

"Good morning, Jules. Late night?"

"Yeah, what's your excuse for sleeping in?"

"I stayed up writing a paper for one of my classes."

"Have you looked outside?"

"No, what's going on?"

"Take a look." Juliane pointed toward the front window. "More snow. I can't believe it's snowing again, and it's still coming down."

Elise went to the window and pushed aside the drape. "But you have to admit it's beautiful."

"You may think so, but I don't." Juliane pouted. "Lukas and I were supposed to go to Cincinnati to a movie this afternoon and dinner tonight."

"I would sympathize, but all I have on my agenda is more schoolwork. So I don't feel sorry for you."

"You're not nice." Juliane picked up a decorative cushion from the couch and tossed it at Elise.

Elise threw her arms up to ward off the pillow that landed at her feet. "Are you forgetting already how I helped when you were sick? I also helped you and Lukas get together."

"I appreciate the care when I was sick, but I hardly think you should take credit for Lukas and me. You probably should share honors with Ferd."

"We both had the right idea, didn't we?"

"You did." Juliane grinned. "Since we've both slept late, I'm going to get dressed, then fix some brunch. How about omelets?"

"Sounds good." Elise headed to the kitchen. "I'll get all the stuff out while you get dressed."

"And I'll call Lukas to see whether we'll still be able to drive to Cincinnati."

When Juliane entered the kitchen a few minutes later, Elise looked up from the stove. "Did you talk to Lukas?"

"No, maybe he's out shoveling snow in Ferd's driveway. I'll try again later."

Juliane and Elise worked together to fix brunch. While they ate, they talked about what was happening at the store and about Elise's classes. Juliane marveled at how well they were getting along with each other. The old rivalries seemed buried. All her worries about living with Elise had never materialized.

As Juliane and Elise cleaned up the kitchen, the doorbell rang. Wondering who would be out on a day like this, Juliane rushed to the front door. When she opened it, Lukas stood on the porch, snow gathering on his dark blue ski jacket and stocking cap.

"Are you going to invite me in, or do I have to stand out here until I look like a snowman?"

"Lukas, what…how did you get over here?"

"I could say in a sleigh with eight tiny reindeer, but I actually made it in my trusty car that I equipped with great tires last fall in an example of brilliant forethought. Are you going to invite me in?"

"I'm sorry." Her heart skipping a beat, she stood aside so he could enter. "I'm just surprised to see you."

Snow fell all over the rug when he stepped inside. He glanced down. "Sorry about that."

"That's okay. Why are you here?"

"Do I have to have an excuse to see my favorite girl?"

Trying to hold back a smile, Juliane let out an exasperated sigh. "You know what I mean. Aren't the roads terrible?"

"The side streets are, but the snowplows have been on the main roads, so they aren't too bad if you take it slow and easy. The main thing is to watch out for the inexperienced drivers."

"You mean there are other crazies out on the roads besides you?"

"Yeah, and I intend to take you out on the road with me."

"You mean we're still going to Cincinnati?"

"No, I have better plans."

"What?"

"Tim and Melanie are taking their boys sledding, and they invited us to come along."

"I don't have a sled."

"I do. Grandpa's a pack rat, and he had my childhood toboggan in his garage."

Juliane laughed. "Are you sure this is a good idea?"

"Absolutely, you've been working overtime at the store, and you need to have a little fun."

"You mean board games until one-thirty in the morning isn't enough fun?"

"No, besides, I promised you a fun day in Cincinnati, and that's not going to work out because of the snow. So we'll take advantage of the snow this way."

Juliane smiled and gave Lukas a little hug and kiss on the cheek. "I think you're right. This does sound like fun."

"Hi, Lukas." Elise walked into the room. "What sounds like fun?"

"Hi, Elise. You want to go sledding with us?"

"Yeah, you should come." Juliane amazed herself as she agreed with the invitation. She wasn't jealous that Lukas invited Elise to join them—one more signal that the old rivalries were dying.

"I'd love to, but I have to study. Midterms."

"Come on, Elise, we haven't been sledding since we were kids."

Elise shook her head. "Maybe another time. You guys go and have fun."

"Okay, then." Juliane glanced down at her jeans and green cable-knit sweater. "Do you think I'm dressed appropriately for this outing?"

"You look pretty good to me." Lukas winked at her.

Juliane put her hands on her hips. "I didn't ask if you liked how I look."

"Okay, I won't tell you that you look fantastically ready for sledding."

"I should've known better than to think you'd give me a straight answer." Juliane headed for the kitchen. There was no doubt. She was falling in love with Lukas. The thought petrified and thrilled her all at the same time. "I'll be back with coat, hat, gloves and boots."

"Great. I'll meet you in the car." Lukas opened the door. "Bye, Elise. Don't study too hard."

As Juliane got bundled up in her gear, Elise joined her in the kitchen. "I think my big sister is falling head over heels."

"You might be right, and it scares me silly."

"Why are you afraid?"

"Isn't love always scary?"

"True. If you ever want to talk about it, I'm here."

"Yeah, and if you ever want to talk about Seth,

same goes for me." Juliane hugged Elise, then raced out to meet Lukas.

After Juliane got in the car and buckled her seat belt, Lukas maneuvered his car down the snowy street. He glanced her way before turning his attention back to the road. "Tim already tested the hill behind their house. He says the sledding is terrific. This ought to be fun. I haven't ridden a toboggan since I was a kid."

"You sound as excited as a kid."

Lukas chuckled. "Wait till I get you on that toboggan."

Tim, Melanie and their children, Andrew and Ryan, were bringing their sleds out of the garage when Lukas pulled into their driveway. While Juliane greeted everyone, he removed the toboggan from his trunk.

"Glad you guys could join us." Tim shook Lukas's hand, then tapped Andrew and Ryan on their heads. "These boys could hardly wait until you got here. So let's head out to the hill."

The group trudged through the snow, dragging their sleds behind them. When they reached the edge of the slope that went down to a stand of trees near a small creek, Tim looked at Lukas. "The slope flattens out a good ways before you get to the trees, but be careful that you don't get going so fast that you can't stop."

Lukas laughed. "Thanks for the warning. Juliane wouldn't appreciate it if I took her for a ride into a tree or the creek."

"That's for sure." Juliane surveyed the toboggan. "Can I trust you to steer this thing?"

"No promises. Just a fun ride. Trust me." Lukas motioned toward the wooden sled. "I'll sit on the back, and you can sit in front of me."

Juliane took a seat with her knees bent. "I hope you know what you're doing."

Lukas sat behind her. "Are you ready?"

"Why do I feel like I'm putting my life in your hands?"

Lukas put his arms around her and grabbed the rope attached to the toboggan. "Don't worry. You're in good hands."

Juliane's heart skittered. "I'm holding you to that."

Next to them the entire Drake family piled onto another toboggan. The little boys shouted for them to go. As they started off down the hill, the boys screamed with delight. Without warning, Lukas shoved off, and Juliane screamed herself as they barreled down the hill behind the Drakes.

When the toboggan swerved sideways, Juliane tumbled into the snow. Lukas hopped off the sled and helped her to her feet. "Are you okay?"

"I think so." She dusted the snow from her pants and coat. "Is that what you call good hands?"

"You didn't wind up in the creek." Lukas put an arm around her shoulders. "Ready to go again?"

"Yeah, but this time give me a little warning before you take off."

"I'll do my best." He saluted and grabbed the sled with one hand, and one of her hands with the other.

As they climbed up the hill for another run, Juliane couldn't help thinking that being with Lukas was the ride of her life. Could she withstand the perils of a relationship with him? Maybe it was too late to be asking that question.

For the rest of the afternoon, Juliane tried not to think of anything except having fun. It wasn't hard to do as they made numerous trips down the hill and later had a playful snowball fight and made snow angels on the hillside.

As the sun sank lower on the horizon, the snow stopped falling, and the sky began to clear. The leafless hardwood trees that surrounded the property were covered in snow. The pinks and oranges created by the setting sun in the dissipating clouds gave an iridescent glow to the landscape. The scene presented a picture worthy of any winter postcard.

Lukas, Tim and the boys started to make a snowman. Lukas looked at Juliane as he rolled a ball of snow for the body. "Aren't you going to help?"

Melanie stepped forward before Juliane could answer. "I've got homemade chili in the slow cooker, so I want you guys to stay for supper. Juliane and I can get things ready while you finish the snowman."

Lukas stopped rolling the ball and straightened. "We don't want to wear out our welcome."

"You can't do that. We'd love to have you. Please say you'll stay."

After checking for Juliane's nod of agreement, Lukas turned back to Melanie. "Hey, I'm not one to refuse some good homemade chili. Thanks." Lukas grinned.

"Great!" Melanie turned to Juliane. "Let's go inside."

Juliane followed Melanie into the house. "Thanks for rescuing me from the cold. I'm not sure I can feel my feet anymore."

"I know what you mean." Smiling, Melanie closed the door. "Do you want to change into some dry clothes? We're about the same size. You can wear something of mine."

"That would be wonderful."

Juliane put on the clothes that Melanie gave her, then went to the kitchen to help. "This has been a wonderful day. Thanks for inviting us."

"I'm so glad you came." Steam rose into the air as Melanie lifted the lid of the slow cooker and stirred the contents.

"I love chili on a cold snowy day. Smells delicious."

"Thanks. Me, too." Melanie took some bowls from the cupboard. "I've wanted to tell you how much Tim and I have enjoyed doing things with you and Lukas the past few weeks."

"We've had a great time, too."

"It's hard to move to a new community where you don't know anyone. So I really appreciate your friendship. The church people are always friendly, but until we started spending time with you and Lukas, I didn't feel as though I had developed any close friends." Melanie laid a hand on Juliane's arm. "I thank God for the times we've spent together and that Lukas is such a good friend and boss to Tim."

"I'm glad you count me as your friend. I grew up in Kellersburg, so I have no idea what it's like to move to a new town."

"You and Lukas seem so happy together. I could see at the Valentine's banquet that he was singing those songs right to you." Melanie got napkins and a box of crackers from the pantry, then turned to Juliane. "I hope you don't mind my asking. Is this a serious relationship?"

Juliane swallowed hard. "We haven't been dating that long."

Seemingly embarrassed, Melanie shook her head. "I'm sorry. I didn't mean to pry or put you on the spot. Sometimes love happens fast and other times it's a slow process. Tim and I knew we were right for each other almost from the first date."

Before Juliane could make a response, noisy feet and voices sounded from the laundry room just off the kitchen as Lukas, Tim and the two boys entered the house.

Juliane couldn't help thinking of Melanie's question and subsequent comments. Juliane knew she was serious about her feelings for Lukas. But loving Lukas meant accepting him and all his flaws. They'd overcome their past, but what about their future? Was their relationship—along with Lukas's faith and commitment to sobriety—strong enough to stand the test of time?

Throughout the rest of the evening, Juliane tried without much success to push troubling thoughts aside. She was going to have to answer that question eventually.

But not today.

Today was all about having fun. She just wanted to enjoy being with Lukas. He loved God, he cared for her and he was good with kids, too. She'd seen that today while he'd played with the two boys.

What else was going to trip her heart and make her care about him more than she already did? Was she willing to take a ride through life with him? Not that he was asking, but where this relationship was headed was something she should consider.

If they continued to date, she had to deal with the reality of future expectations. And those expectations were barreling down on her like the toboggans that had rushed down the hill today.

But why should she borrow trouble from tomorrow? Didn't Lukas have to take one day at a time? So should she. Everything about today had been perfect. Life was good. What could happen to change that?

The loud jangling awakened Lukas from his sleep. Sitting up in bed, he wiped a hand down his face. He grabbed his BlackBerry from the bedside stand. As he answered the call, the lighted face on the BlackBerry told him it was five o'clock in the morning. The caller ID indicated that the call was coming from Tim Drake. Was something wrong at the plant?

"Lukas Frey here."

"Lukas, this is Melanie Drake." Lukas couldn't miss the distress in her voice. "I didn't know who else to call. Can you…" Her voice trailed off as she began to cry.

Lukas's heart sank. "Melanie, what's wrong?"

"Something's wrong with Tim. I'm at the hospital. Can you come?"

"I'll be there as soon as I get dressed."

"Thank you."

His heart pounding and a sick feeling in his stomach, Lukas jumped out of bed and grabbed a pair of jeans and a sweater. He pulled on a pair of socks on his way to the door. Opening the door to the garage, he grabbed his coat and shoved his feet into the shoes that he'd left by the door. As he drove through the darkness, he relived the night when the ambulance had taken his grandfather to the hospital. He prayed that Tim would be okay.

When Lukas arrived, he found Melanie in the emergency room, along with Ryan and Andrew. The poor little boys were half-asleep. The stress of the situation plus having to drag her children to the emergency room showed on her face. His heart went out to her.

As soon as Melanie saw him, she rushed over. "Thank you so much for coming."

"I'm glad to help however I can. Do you know what's wrong?"

Melanie shook her head, tears welling in her eyes. "The doctors are still examining him."

Lukas put an arm around Melanie's shoulders and tried to comfort her. "Would you like for me to say a prayer?"

She nodded. Lukas led her to the chairs where the boys were sitting. They held hands in a circle while he prayed for Tim. After they finished praying, Lukas looked up. "If I call Juliane, she could take the boys back home, so they don't have to sit here. Do you think they'd go with her?"

"You don't have to disturb her."

"She won't mind, and the boys should be comfort-

able with her since we watched them the other night."
Lukas knew he could count on Juliane.

"I'll see." Melanie talked softly with Ryan and
Andrew, then looked over at Lukas with a nod.
"That'll be fine."

Lukas called Juliane and explained the situation.
She immediately agreed to come for Andrew and Ryan.

When Juliane arrived, Lukas met her at the
entrance and gave her a hug. He wanted to keep her
in his embrace, but this wasn't the time. "Thanks so
much for doing this."

"You know if you ever need anything, I'm there.
Do you know anything about Tim's condition yet?"

Lukas shook his head, knowing Juliane's statement
went beyond this current problem. She would be there
for him no matter what because she loved him. In the
past two weeks she had made that abundantly clear.
He still had a hard time believing what a lucky man
he was. "I'm reliving that night with Grandpa."

"I thought of that as soon as you told me." Juliane
went over to Melanie and gave her a hug. Then Lukas
helped Juliane take the boys to her car.

After they buckled the children into the backseat,
she turned and gave Lukas a kiss on the cheek. "Take
care of Melanie. I'll be praying."

"Thanks." He blew her a kiss and thanked God
that he had found her.

While he walked back to the emergency room, he

thought about the night barely two weeks ago when the two of them had watched Ryan and Andrew while Tim and Melanie had gone out to celebrate their tenth anniversary. Sharing that time with Juliane made him want a family of his own more than ever, and she was part of that dream.

Just as Lukas returned to the waiting area, a physician in a white coat escorted Melanie through the swinging double doors. Lukas prayed and paced as he waited to hear the news. In a few minutes, Melanie walked back through the doors. Her grim expression caused a lump to form in his throat. When she saw him, she burst into tears and covered her face with her hands. Rushing to her side, he gathered her in his arms. She blubbered something against his chest. In the almost unintelligible sentence, he understood two words.

Aneurysm.

Died.

His heart sank to his stomach. A churning sensation hit him in the gut while a cold, numb feeling settled around his heart. He took a shaky breath as Melanie clung to him and wept. How was he going to comfort her when he was hurting so badly himself?

Chapter Fifteen

Shivering in the cold confines of his car, Lukas gripped the steering wheel. The day had been rotten. The past two weeks had been even worse. Sorrow over Tim's death still weighed him down. He'd never had a good friend like Tim. They'd only known each other for a few months, but it had seemed as though they had known each other for years. Now he was gone, leaving a huge void.

The red-and-white neon sign advertising the beer Lukas used to drink beckoned to him from the pub's window two doors down the block. While he relished the taste of a cold draft beer, he could still see the casket and the stricken faces of Tim's widow, Melanie, and her two boys, so solemn and brave in their little suits and ties. The scene tore him up inside. A crushing sensation filled his chest as he swallowed the lump that formed in his throat and made him feel as though he couldn't breathe.

The extra responsibilities at work and the pain of losing his good friend made Lukas want a beer in the worst way. He'd managed to get through helping Melanie with the funeral arrangements and the funeral itself without the need for a drink. But the cumulative effect of all that had happened was beginning to bring him down, and the need for a drink became stronger every day.

His thoughts played good-cop, bad-cop. The bad cop kept telling him that a couple of beers would ease the tension and take the edge off his problems. Just two tonight and then he'd go back on the wagon. The good cop told him he was a fool to believe that he could stop with two.

Lukas knew which one was right, but he didn't want to listen. The pain was too great. Even thoughts of Juliane didn't take away the hurt or the desire for that beer.

Why had God allowed Melanie and her boys to lose their husband and father? Tim's death brought back all the anguish Lukas had dealt with when his mother had died.

God hadn't been there for Tim, and God wasn't helping Lukas now. His prayers went unanswered.

Lukas got out of his car and pocketed his keys. His breath created a cloud in the night air. Still warring with himself, he stood on the sidewalk and stared at the blinking sign. What would be the harm? He'd order a burger and fries and wash them down with a couple of beers. That was the plan.

Shoving his hands in his coat pockets, Lukas strode toward the pub. As he reached for the door handle, a car honked and he turned to look. A movement across the street caught his eye as a man lurched away from the curb in front of Keller's Variety. He stumbled down the walk, then stopped and leaned against the brick building. In the store window, a mannequin dressed in a spring outfit mocked the cold surrounding him.

In the darkness, Lukas tried to figure out what was wrong with the man. Was he ill, or was he drunk? Lukas hurried across the street to assist him. When Lukas reached the man's side, he took his arm. Then he looked into his face.

Juliane's father—Ray Keller.

Shock stabbed Lukas in the heart when he smelled the alcohol on Ray's breath. Gazing into Ray's eyes, Lukas had no doubt that the man was drunk. What was going on? Lukas swallowed hard. He'd never known that Juliane's father drank anything stronger than cola. What was he going to do?

Contemplating what this would mean for Juliane, Lukas managed to steer Ray across the street toward the car. Lukas helped Ray into the passenger seat and realized that the older man didn't recognize him or know where they were.

Lukas stared at Ray's slack jaw and glassy eyes. Was that the way he'd looked when he'd been drunk? The picture created a sick feeling in the pit of his stomach. "Ray, do you want me to take you home?"

Ray looked up, his head wobbling like a bobble head. He seemed to try to focus. Then he started to weep and talk at the same time, his words slurred. "Don't take me home. Barbara will be upset. I'm so sorry."

Lukas closed the car door and went around to the driver's side and got in. As he sat there wondering what to do, the neon beer sign caught his eye again. He'd almost given in to temptation and thrown away everything he'd worked for over the past six years. At that moment, he knew God had saved him by providing a wake-up call. He felt like weeping the same as Ray but for a whole different reason—gratitude to God. Lukas knew he'd been wrong. God was there. He'd been there the whole time.

If he hadn't been tempted to have a drink tonight, he wouldn't have been here to see Ray and help him. *And we know that in all things God works for the good of those who love Him, who have been called according to His purpose.* The scripture from Romans that Lukas had memorized ran through his mind.

Lukas started his car and headed for his home, where he planned to have Ray sleep it off. When

Lukas reached the house, he helped Juliane's father inside and into the guest room. Lukas wanted the man to explain the situation, but this wasn't the time. Ray needed to be sober for that talk.

While getting Ray settled in the guest room, Lukas thought of the estrangement with his own father. Their parting wasn't bitter, but Lukas had let that relationship deteriorate while he'd been drinking heavily. Once he was sober, he didn't know how to repair it. Maybe the time had come.

Ray started snoring as soon as he hit the bed. Lukas shut off the light and went into the living room. Plopping on the couch, he worried about Juliane's reaction. Should he call her? Surely Barbara would be concerned when Ray didn't come home. He had to call Juliane.

When Lukas heard Juliane's voice, his stomach clenched. "Hi. How are you?"

"Good. Is your meeting at the plant done?"

"Yeah." Lukas hesitated. "I need to talk to you about something, and I don't want to do it over the phone."

"You want to come over?"

"No. There's something *here* I have to show you."

"What?"

"You'll see when you get here."

Ending the call, Lukas hoped he was doing the right thing.

While he waited for Juliane to arrive, he paced.

He tried to figure out how he was going to approach this problem. He stopped in his tracks. God had helped him tonight. Why wasn't he praying about this, too? Bowing his head, Lukas prayed until he heard the doorbell.

He raced to the door. "Thanks for coming."

"You've been too busy. I've missed you." Putting her arms around his neck, she kissed him.

When the kiss ended, he held her tight and let his chin rest on the top of her head. He knew how close he'd come to ruining their relationship, but what he was about to tell her could damage it just as much. "I've missed you, too."

She stepped out of his embrace. "What do you have to show me?"

Lukas wished this was all a bad dream. "Come sit on the couch."

Juliane joined Lukas and sat there with expectation written all over her face. "Okay, show me."

"First, I have to ask you something."

"Okay."

Lukas had no idea how to phrase the question. Finally, he blurted, "Has your father ever been drunk?"

Her eyes grew wide as the color drained from her face. "Why would you ask that?"

"Follow me." Lukas stood and went down the short hallway to the guest room. He opened the door and stepped aside as the hallway light illuminated the snoring figure on the bed. "I found him tonight outside your store, barely able to stand."

"Not again." Her words came out in a soft cry. Leaning back against the wall, Juliane lowered her head and placed a hand on her forehead.

"So this has happened before?"

She nodded but wouldn't look at him. She pushed away from the wall and walked back to the living room without saying a word. He wanted to rush after her and pull her into his arms and comfort her. But part of him was angry—angry that she hadn't been willing to share this with him.

When she reached the living room, she pulled her BlackBerry out of her purse. "I have to call my mother."

While Juliane talked to her mother, Lukas fumed. He wanted answers.

After she finished talking, she looked at him with a detached expression as if she was trying to void herself of all emotion. "I'll take him home."

Lukas shook his head. "He's asleep. I'll bring him home in the morning."

"Okay." She jammed her BlackBerry into her purse and picked up her coat. "I'll be going then."

With both hands, Lukas grabbed her by the shoulders. "Juliane, talk to me about this."

She refused to look at him. "I can't."

"Why?" Dropping his hands, Lukas pointed to himself. "Me of all people. I would understand."

"I wanted to tell you—to talk about it. But I couldn't bring myself to do it. I was too embarrassed. I've been keeping this secret for so long, I just—"

"If this has been going on for a long time, your father needs help."

"Don't you think I know that?" Blinking back tears, she looked up. "But you ought to know that you can't help someone until they want it."

"You're right, but with my experience, I might have been able to get through to him. If you refuse to tell people about his problem, you'll never be able to find anyone to help him."

"The way you told people about *your* problem? Admit it, you didn't want to let anyone in town know about your past. You hid it, just like my mother and I have been hiding my father's drinking problems for years. If I hadn't already known, you wouldn't have told me."

Her comment stung. He'd been kidding himself, thinking that this relationship was going somewhere. He loved Juliane, but she didn't love him enough to trust him. And the worst part was wondering if she was right. He'd been honest with her…but was it only because she already knew the worst? "I can't believe you said that after all the things I've shared with you. I thought we loved each other, but you're shutting me out."

"I don't know what I'm doing. I can't deal with

you or my father right now. Please leave me alone."
Sobbing, she ran from the house, the door slamming
behind her.

Lukas stood there staring at the door. She might
as well have slammed his heart in it. Anguish pressed
down on him, giving him a hopeless feeling that
made him long for a drink. But he remembered how
Ray had looked tonight. Lukas knew he didn't want
to go down that path no matter how much he hurt. A
bottle of beer wouldn't help him. God was his hope.
And with God's help, he'd find a way to mend his
broken heart.

A month later, Juliane sat at her kitchen table while
she sipped hot tea and nibbled on a piece of toast.
Elise hummed a contemporary hymn as she poured
some tea and made a big bowl of cereal.

Elise brought her food to the table. "Did you hear?
Mom invited Lukas to join us for Dad's getting-out-
of-rehab celebration lunch today."

Juliane almost choked on the toast. She quickly
drank some tea to help wash it down.

Elise grinned at her. "I thought that would get a
reaction."

"I suppose you think that's great."

"I do. It's time you quit trying to avoid Lukas."

"You should be the last person to lecture me about
relationships."

"You're right, but I hate seeing you so miserable. You've lost weight because you never eat."

"Did it ever occur to you that I'm working so hard to make up for Dad being away from the store that I don't have time to eat?"

"Funny how your loss of appetite started right after you quit seeing Lukas."

"We've been through this before. Nothing's changed, so let's not rehash it."

Elise sighed. "Okay, but I hope for Dad's sake you can be civil to Lukas."

"I can be civil. I just don't want a relationship with him."

"I think you're kidding yourself. You still love him no matter what you say."

"You can believe what you like." Trying to deny the truth of Elise's assertion, Juliane put her dishes in the dishwasher and headed for her bedroom. "I'll be leaving for church in fifteen minutes."

"I'll be ready." Elise stopped Juliane at the door. "I don't understand why things went wrong between you and Lukas, but I wish you wouldn't let what happened with Dad stand between you. Lukas understands. After all, he helped convince Dad to go into rehab."

"One day I hope you'll understand." Hurrying to get away from Elise's lectures, Juliane wanted so much to explain her fight with Lukas, but she couldn't. Especially since Lukas had been right. Once he'd known the truth, Lukas had been able to convince her father to get help. If she'd been open about her father's problem earlier, maybe he'd have sought treatment years earlier. She bore the blame for not getting her father the help that he needed, and she couldn't bear the thought of facing Lukas while she believed that he blamed her, too.

Juliane sat in the back pew and tried not to look at Lukas, who was in the choir loft. She'd stopped singing in the choir because of the extra load at work and also to avoid Lukas, but her gaze was drawn to him almost against her will. For the first time, she found him looking back. Her heart tripped.

Everything Elise had said to Juliane this morning crowded into her mind. She couldn't deny that she still loved Lukas, but on the night of their argument the pain and embarrassment had overwhelmed her, and she had run.

Run from her feelings.

Run from her fears.

Her dad's celebration lunch would compel her to face them.

She should quit noticing Lukas and pay attention to the sermon. As the pastor concluded his sermon on spiritual gifts, he motioned toward someone in the audience. Melanie Drake and Lukas both approached the pulpit.

"Two of our members come today to tell you how they are using their gifts to start special ministries to assist others." After the pastor's introduction, Melanie stepped up and talked about the people who helped her after her husband's death. She explained her plans for a grief recovery group. When she finished, the church elders prayed for this new ministry.

After the prayers, Lukas stepped to the pulpit. "Hello, my name is Lukas, and I'm an alcoholic."

A murmur rolled through the congregation. A lump rose in Juliane's throat as Lukas proceeded. "That statement has shocked some of you, but I wanted to share my struggles so you'll understand why I'm starting a recovery group for people who have experienced substance abuse. God calls us to help each other, but if we don't share our problems, no one can help. I'd like to read a couple of scriptures. First, Galatians 6:1–2. 'Brothers, if someone is caught in a sin, you who are spiritual should restore him gently. But watch yourself, or you also may be tempted. Carry each other's burdens, and in this way you will fulfill the law of Christ.'

"And Hebrews 3:13. 'But encourage one another daily, as long as it is called Today, so that none of you may be hardened by sin's deceitfulness.'"

Lukas closed his Bible. "When I moved to Kellersburg you welcomed me, but I was afraid to let you know about my alcoholism. That was a mistake. I realize now that you need to know my problem so you can help carry my burden. And I want to help others like a dear friend helped me by showing me God's grace and mercy. I thank God every day for him.

"My fight is a daily one. Please pray for me. I can't do this by myself. I need God's strength and your encouragement. Knowing that you are praying will help me. I also want you to hold me accountable. I don't want to return to my old way of life. Recently, I almost slipped, but God gave me a way out of the temptation as He has promised. And please pray for this ministry and Melanie's."

As the elders prayed for Lukas's ministry, Juliane felt as though a large stone sat on her chest, pressing all the air out of her lungs. After all her accusations, Lukas had shown more bravery than she'd ever possessed by openly acknowledging his problems and asking for help—the very things she had been unwilling to do. His example humbled her.

She'd hurt Lukas. Could he ever forgive her? She had to ask for his forgiveness and hope that he'd give her another chance. As the prayer ended, Juliane's heart raced as her parents walked hand in hand down the aisle and up to the stage where Lukas stood.

Ray shook Lukas's hand, then stepped to the pulpit. "My name is Ray, and I'm an alcoholic."

Tears blurred Juliane's vision as her father looked over the congregation. After all these years, her father had finally gotten help, no thanks to her. Now, because of Lukas, her dad would have a support group, and others in the community could find help here, too. She grabbed a tissue from her purse and wiped her eyes and nose. When her dad started to speak, a lump rose in her throat.

Ray gripped the edges of the pulpit. "I thank God today that this young man had the courage to tell me that I needed help. As you've learned, he knows from experience what it's like to have an addiction. I believe God brought him here as the answer to a lot of prayers. I've learned that even though people were timid about telling me what I needed, they were praying for me."

Juliane thought about her dad's statement. She'd been praying for years that her father would quit drinking forever. Was Lukas part of the answer to those prayers?

As her dad finished speaking, she met Lukas's gaze. When he didn't look away, her heart filled with hope. Maybe he would give her another chance at love.

After the closing prayer, many in the congregation greeted Melanie, Lukas and Ray. Despite the positive indicator she'd read in Lukas's look, Juliane wasn't sure how to respond. But she gathered her courage as she made her way through the crowd to see her dad, knowing it might mean talking with Lukas, as well.

When she reached her dad, she went into his arms,

and he held her tight. "Daddy, I'm so proud of you and happy for you."

"Thanks for your prayers, Jules."

As her dad released her, she blinked back more tears. Her heart swelled with love.

Elise pulled Juliane aside. "Now I understand what you've been going through. How are you feeling about it today?"

"I'm going to talk to him. I'm praying he'll agree to a new start." Juliane glanced at Lukas, who still had a crowd around him, including Ferd. "Looks like I'm going to have to wait my turn."

"You go get 'im." Elise gave Juliane a quick hug. "I'll go ahead with Mom and Dad to the restaurant. I'll be praying, too."

"Thanks. I'll see you in a little bit."

Standing off to the side, Juliane wished the crowd would disperse, but several folks lingered as they continued to talk to Lukas. Finally, she decided to go to the parking lot to wait by his car.

As she left the building, the April sunshine put cheer in her heart. Daffodils in the church flower beds trumpeted the arrival of spring—a promise of new beginnings. Everything around her conveyed optimism.

Could she have a new beginning with Lukas?

Every time someone came out the side door that led to the parking lot, Juliane's stomach churned. Each time that person wasn't Lukas, her heart sank.

She mentally rehearsed her speech while anticipation jumbled her insides, making her apprehensive. Closing her eyes, she took a deep breath. The fresh spring air had a calming effect until she opened her eyes and saw Lukas striding toward her.

Her breath caught in her throat as her pulse throbbed. She felt as though her heart were beating on the outside of her chest. Everything she'd rehearsed escaped her mind. She swallowed hard, but her tongue wouldn't work.

Lukas smiled, but she still couldn't speak.

"Are you okay?" Jingling his keys in his pocket, he stopped beside her. "You look a little peaked."

Scared silly was more like it, not for the old reason but scared that he'll say no. She took another deep breath. "I'm fine, but I'd be a whole lot finer if you'd forgive me for the way I acted about my dad and let me start over with you. I was totally wrong, and you were so right and so brave about my dad. And I'm so proud of you and your ministry. And I can't thank you enough for everything you've done."

He didn't say anything, just stared at her while she fought against threatening tears. Dying inside, she started to turn away.

Lukas gently took her arm. "In that big long speech you forgot to say one thing."

Turning back, she swallowed a big lump in her throat. "What?"

"I still love you." He pulled her into his arms. "I still love you, Juliane, and I forgive you. Do you still love me?"

She held him tight. "I still love you, too, and I never want to let you go."

He laughed. "I hope you let me go long enough for us to join your dad's celebration."

Relief washing over her, Juliane released her hold and laced her hands behind his neck. She gazed up at him. "I love you, Lukas. I never stopped loving you, but I had some lessons to learn. So does this mean you're willing to start over?"

"You're sure that's what you want? You're willing to put up with me and my faults?"

"As long as you're willing to put up with mine."

"We can try to understand each other, but let's *not* start over—"

"But I thought you said—"

He put a finger to her lips. "Let me finish. I don't want to go all the way back. Let's start from here and go forward."

"I like your plan."

"One more thing before we go." Lukas leaned over and brushed his lips against hers.

Juliane pulled him closer and kissed him back, her heart believing in a promise for the future.

* * * * *

Dear Reader,

Hometown Promise is the first book in a three-book series set in my imaginary town of Kellersburg, Ohio. The area of Ohio in and around Cincinnati is special to me because I met my husband in Cincinnati. We were married in Madeira and had our reception in Loveland. Could that be the reason we've been married for over thirty years? Our two daughters were born while we lived in this area. So I decided that my story should have two sisters, Juliane and Elise Keller. Although these sisters aren't based on my daughters and have little resemblance to them, I wanted to explore Juliane and Elise's relationship in light of the story of the prodigal son that we read about in Luke 15.

I hope you enjoyed reading about Juliane and Lukas. Their story shows us how we can rely on God to help us with the family dynamics that can impact our lives.

I love to hear from readers. I enjoy your letters and e-mails so much. You can write to me at P.O. Box 16461, Fernandina Beach, Florida 32035, or through my Web site: www.merrilleewhren.com.

May God bless you,

Merrillee Whren

QUESTIONS FOR DISCUSSION

1. At the beginning of the story Juliane has an unfavorable view of Lukas. Why? Do you think her view is justified? Do you think she handled the situation correctly? How would you have handled it?

2. Lukas is worried about how he will be accepted in this new town. He worries that people will find out about his past. Do you think this is a legitimate fear? How would you feel if you were in his situation?

3. Juliane is concerned about her sister's return. Why? Compare what happens between Juliane and Elise and the story of the prodigal son found in the fifteenth chapter of Luke.

4. What problem does Juliane's father have? How does she deal with it? Do you think she did the right thing? Why or why not?

5. What incident first gives Juliane a different view of Lukas? Why do you think this changed her mind about him? Have you ever known someone who did something that changes your opinion about them for better or worse? Explain.

6. Juliane and Elise discover that they are envious of each other. Why do you think people look at others with envy? Have you or someone you know ever had this problem? How can this problem be handled?

7. Lukas began drinking to fit in. Have you or someone you know ever done anything to fit in but found that it ultimately didn't help and may have hurt? Explain.

8. Lukas was glad to move to Kellersburg, in part to be near his grandfather because he is dealing with numerous health issues. Do you or someone you know have an elderly relative who has health issues? How have you been able to help with these problems?

9. Juliane has difficulty dealing with the envious thoughts she has regarding her sister. How do the following scriptures from Romans 12:9–10, Romans 13:8–9, James 3:13–18 and 1 John 4:19–21 relate to her problem?

10. During the blizzard, Juliane's parents lose electrical power. Have you ever been in a storm that caused the loss of electrical power or some other problem? What kind of storm was it? How did

you deal with the problems? Did you pray? If so, how did the prayers help?

11. When Tim Drake dies suddenly, Lukas is deeply affected. How does this complicate his life? Has someone close to you died unexpectedly? If so, how did this affect your life? How did you deal with it?

12. After Lukas nearly succumbs to the temptation to have a drink, he realizes how God made a way of escape from the temptation. What temptations do you find most troublesome? Have you found God making a way of escape for you? Explain.

13. Melanie and Lukas start ministries to help people in their church and community. How are they especially suited for the ministries they started? What kind of gifts do you have that lend themselves to a ministry? Why does sharing our problems with others help us? How is this a Biblical principle?

14. When Lukas discovers Ray's drinking problem, what does he realize about Juliane? Why does Lukas feel anger? Do you think he handled the situation correctly? How do you view Juliane's reaction? Have you ever had a secret that you couldn't share? Explain.

15. What finally makes Juliane realize she has been wrong about the way she has been handling her relationship with Lukas and her father? Have you or someone you know ever found you have been wrong about the way you have dealt with a problem? Explain.

Read on for a sneak preview of
KATIE'S REDEMPTION
by Patricia Davids,
the first book in the heartwarming new
BRIDES OF AMISH COUNTRY series
available in March 2010
from Steeple Hill Love Inspired.

When a pregnant formerly Amish woman
returns to her brother's house, seeking
forgiveness and a place to give birth
to her child, what she finds there
isn't what she expected.

*P*lease, God, don't let them send me away.

To give her child a home Katie Lantz would endure the angry tirade she expected from her brother. Through it all Malachi wouldn't be able to hide the gloating in his voice.

An unexpected tightening across her stomach made Katie suck in a quick breath. She'd been up since dawn, riding for hours on the jolting bus.

Her stomach tightened again. The pain deepened. Something wasn't right. This was more than fatigue. It was labor.

Breathing hard, she peered through the blowing snow. It wasn't much farther to her brother's farm. Closing her eyes, she gathered her strength.

One foot in front of the other. The only way to finish a journey is to start it.

She sagged with relief when her hand closed over the railing. She was home.

Home. The word echoed inside her mind, bringing with it unhappy memories that pushed aside her relief. Raising her fist, she knocked at the front door. Then she bowed her head and closed her eyes, grasping the collar of her coat to keep the chill at bay.

When the door finally opened, she looked up to meet her brother's gaze.

Katie sucked in a breath and then took a half step back. A tall, broad-shouldered Amish man stood in front of her with a kerosene lamp in his hand and a faintly puzzled expression on his handsome face.

It wasn't Malachi.

To read more of Katie's story,
pick up KATIE'S REDEMPTION
by Patricia Davids,
available March 2010.

Love Inspired® SUSPENSE

RIVETING INSPIRATIONAL ROMANCE

Watch for our new series of
edge-of-your-seat suspense novels.
These contemporary tales
of intrigue and romance
feature Christian characters
facing challenges to their faith...
and their lives!

NOW AVAILABLE IN REGULAR & LARGER-PRINT FORMATS

Steeple
Hill®

Visit:
www.SteepleHill.com